## "Are you propo[sing]
## Elin asked

Her voice was low and furious. She felt raw inside with the angry emotions he had unleashed in her.

Garel laughed. "What a touching display of outraged virtue."

Elin stared at him. She saw the way his gleaming hair fell carelessly on to his swarthy forehead, the aggressive thrust of his jaw, his stern nose with the expressively flared nostrils. His mouth was hard, and in his face, there was a ruthless air of purpose.

"Get out!" she hissed.

His chiseled expression revealed very little except for the glitter of satisfaction in his eyes.

"Yes, I'll get out of your house," he said. "But don't expect me to get out of your life, because I'm no longer convinced that what was between us is over."

**JENNY ARDEN**, a British writer, combines a career as a college lecturer in business studies with the writing she has always wanted to do. Her favorite place for relaxation is North Wales, but travel fascinates her—both the places she has visited and the places she dreams about for future journeying. In her spare time, she enjoys sculpting historical figures in clay and cooking for company. Huckleberry, her Burmese Blue cat, is her companion while writing. He usually sits in a chair beside the typewriter, but occasionally, in a fit of jealousy, will bid for her attention by sitting on the keys!

## Books by Jenny Arden

HARLEQUIN PRESENTS
1063—TO THE VICTOR, THE SPOILS
1215—FRIEND OR FOE
1311—THIS TIME, FOREVER

HARLEQUIN ROMANCE
2995—SOME ENCHANTING EVENING
3115—ARROGANT INVADER

# JENNY ARDEN

## running scared

*Harlequin Books*

TORONTO • NEW YORK • LONDON
AMSTERDAM • PARIS • SYDNEY • HAMBURG
STOCKHOLM • ATHENS • TOKYO • MILAN

Harlequin Presents first edition October 1991
ISBN 0-373-11399-4

Original hardcover edition published in 1990
by Mills & Boon Limited

RUNNING SCARED

# CHAPTER ONE

WHEN Elin had learned that the repair work on her car wouldn't be finished till after the weekend, she had debated phoning her accountant to tell him that she wouldn't be able to make his housewarming party after all. But now, mingling easily with the other guests on the lawn, she didn't regret having come.

James, unable to spend as much time with her as he'd have liked to because of his duties as host, found his gaze straying to her. She was standing chatting to a group of his friends, and he could hear the sound of their laughter.

It was a sultry evening, the city sky thundery after a blazingly hot day that had sent the temperature in London suddenly soaring into the eighties. Yet, in a red taffeta dress with a short ruched skirt, she had never looked more bewitchingly cool.

Her dark hair cascaded over her bare shoulders, while equally dark lashes fringed eyes that were a pure emerald-green. Gold hoop earrings danced against her cheeks, and a heavy gold bracelet adorned one slender wrist. She not only had style, she possessed grace, poise, an attractive sense of humour and a maddening quality of independence. Not for the first time, James wondered what he could do to get their relationship on to the sort of basis he wanted.

When he joined her some while later she was with the same chattering group.

'I've been looking for you,' he began.

'I've been right here all along,' she said, her green eyes gently teasing as she lifted her head to look at him.

James smiled, his eyes lingering on her face. 'Among the crush I couldn't locate you immediately,' he said.

'I'd no idea you were giving such a big party.'

'I believe in doing things on a grand scale,' James joked. 'Anyway, are you enjoying yourself?'

'Very much,' she answered truthfully, glad he didn't know how nearly she had cancelled.

At twenty-five, she was less gregarious than she had been once. Generally she much preferred an informal evening with a few friends to large parties, although, in any case, the business she ran kept her too busy to have time for a very active social life.

Not that she objected. She told herself that she was over the trauma of splitting up with her husband. Yet, two years on, the memories of her marriage were still painful, and the elusiveness that James found so beguiling masked a determination never to get involved in another relationship.

His hand at her elbow, James said, 'Come inside for a while. There's someone I want you to meet.'

'I don't think I can remember any more names,' she replied with her attractive laugh as he guided her across the patio where couples were dancing to the sounds of Fleetwood Mac.

'One more won't make any difference, and this is a friend of mine from university days.'

'Male or female?' she teased.

'Now would I make you jealous by introducing you to one of my lady-friends?' he protested.

'Since you're never short of female company,' she

smiled, 'it's just as well I'm *not* jealous.'

'You should be pleased that I like the fair sex,' he quipped. 'It's why I appreciate you so much.'

She laughed, and together they went through the french windows and into the house. The atmosphere in his spacious drawing-room was noisy with conversation and faintly tinged with cigarette smoke. She was wondering whom it was among the press of people that James especially wanted to introduce her to, when her gaze fell on the man who was talking to a pretty Nordic-type blonde she'd seen earlier on the patio.

Some sixth sense made the skin at the back of her neck prickle uneasily. The man's back was to her, the way he held his dark head adding to an aloof bearing that bordered on arrogance. His expensively tailored dinner-jacket emphasised the powerful line of his shoulders, while his stance conveyed both authority and self-possession.

In sudden consternation she fought to deny what instinct told her. Surely it was an illusion? She had to be mistaken. Yet one glimpse of the man's tall, lithe frame across the crowded room was enough for her to be certain she recognised him.

Her heart began to race. Only vaguely was she aware of James's hand against her back as he guided her towards the other couple. Not once in five years had she ever mistaken anyone for Garel, not even briefly, so there was no reason for her to think she was wrong now. She was filled with dismay; the impulse rose up in her to turn and run before any meeting could be forced on her.

But there wasn't time for escape. There wasn't even time to brace herself mentally, for at that moment the man turned his head.

She caught her breath, a faint surge of colour coming into her face as she met the flinty directness of his dark gaze. Her senses had warned her rightly. It was Garel! The years rolled away as, for an instant that seemed to defeat time, she stared back at him.

The other guests, the lazy throb of the music, James standing at her side, all receded like so many shadows so that the only person in focus was the tanned, strongly featured man in front of her, who was looking at her with a satirical glitter of recognition in his brown eyes.

James's genial voice forced her to rally from the first shock of disbelief.

'Elin, I want you to meet a business associate and old friend of mind. Garel, this is——'

'There's no need for an introduction,' she put in quickly before he could finish. Out of pride alone she refused to have Garel learn she had gone back to her maiden name, that she was now divorced from the man she had eventually married.

'That's right. Elin and I already know each other,' Garel confirmed smoothly while his dark gaze continued to slash her.

Familiar with his charismatic Welsh voice, she caught the edge of mockery in it. Anger welled up inside her, and her fingers tightened on her glass with the effort of stopping herself from dashing the last of its contents in his good-looking swarthy face.

Yet James clearly detected none of the sudden flaring of static in the atmosphere. With a half-smile of puzzlement, he said, 'How come the two of you are acquainted? I'd no idea.'

'Garel worked for my father at one time,' Elin told

him, staggered that she could sound so collected and composed when she felt so horribly shaken. She glanced at her cocktail glass and remarked carelessly, 'I think I'd like another Martini.'

'Wait here and I'll get it for you,' James offered promptly, taking her glass from her.

She saw the gleam of cynical amusement in Garel's eyes and her own sparked in return. Damn him, she thought savagely. Quite obviously he'd guessed that it had been her intention to use the pretext of fetching a drink to escape him.

Allowing her no opportunity to beat a retreat, his hand closed on her elbow, making her stiffen. Forestalling the blonde who was on the point of making a bid to reclaim his exclusive attention, he murmured urbanely, 'Excuse us.'

Though his hold was light, Elin could sense the steel-like strength in his fingers. If she made the least attempt to pull away she knew his grip would tighten cruelly in order to thwart her.

Angry that he had hijacked her, she challenged in a fierce desire to shame him, 'Aren't you going to introduce me to your wife?'

His dark eyebrows came together as he gave her a considering look. 'What makes you think I'm married?'

'*Aren't* you?' she retorted, a smouldering light in her green eyes.

'No, I'm not.'

His clipped answer had the ring of sincerity to it. Her mistrustful gaze swung away from his chiselled features as she speculated on his reply. It was possible that he was now divorced. In fact, with his standards or morality it was highly probable! Presumably his wife had finally found out about his casual affairs.

Antagonism welled up in her more furiously with her thoughts, and she made an attempt to snatch her arm away from him. His iron grip thwarted her.

'Let go of me!' she hissed.

'Is that all you can say to me after all these years?' he mocked, his mouth quirking cynically.

Tilting her chin to a regal angle, she answered coldly, 'Frankly, I'm surprised you even remember me. I would have thought you had far too many women in your life for me to have made *any* lasting impression on you!'

'But *you* were something special,' he gibed, before asking, 'So where's Roger this evening?'

She was furious at his insult, and his question caught her unawares. Bluffing quickly, she managed, 'He . . . he couldn't be with me tonight.'

'Do you make a habit of going to parties without your husband?' Garel enquired.

'That's none of your business!'

'Well, as you don't want to talk about your marriage,' he said, with a slight edge of sarcasm, 'why don't you tell me what you're doing here in London?'

She fought to bring her emotions under control, amazed at how badly meeting him again had jolted her, and determined not to let him see it. When she had ended their briefer-than-brief affair she had deliberately left him with the impression that she was his equal when it came to being hard and unprincipled. If now she allowed him to guess that she was completely unnerved by their unexpected encounter, he would know it had all been an act.

'I live here,' she answered. 'And what is this, an interrogation?'

'Why so hostile, Elin?' he taunted. 'I'd almost think that after all this time I still mean something to you.'

A flash of fury went through her. Concealing it, she said, shading her tone with derision, 'You *never* meant anything to me. Did you hope that you had?' His grip tightened as she spoke, his fingers biting into her skin, careless that they hurt her. Reacting instinctively, she flared, 'You're hurting me! Now take your hands off me before I make a scene.'

'Go ahead,' he replied.

Her stormy green eyes warred with his, resentment burning in her as he dared her to have the temerity to carry out her threat. Then, unable to sustain his gaze, she let her dark lashes flutter down, emphasising the becoming tinge of angry colour in her cheeks.

As she conceded defeat, Garel's punishing grip eased. His voice held a low sneer as he mocked, 'You haven't changed much, have you? You always did hate the thought of gossip.'

'And doubtless you haven't changed much either,' she retaliated. 'I expect you're still the same practised liar!'

'I think you'd better explain that remark.'

There was a biting note in Garel's voice that cautioned her. In his black dinner-jacket he looked elegant and suave. But, for all his gentleman's appearance, it had been a pirate who had stared her down an instant ago, and it was a pirate's ruthlessness she saw in his face now.

She was relieved to catch sight of James, who was weaving his way across the crowded room towards them. Bravado flowed back into her and, with a defiant tilt to her chin, she answered, 'I don't have to explain anything to you.'

James's interruption appeared to give her the victory of having the last word.

'One Martini, as requested,' he smiled, handing her glass to her. 'Have you had anything to eat, Garel? There's still plenty of the buffet left.'

'I'll get myself a plate,' Garel answered. He crossed in front of Elin, touching her shoulder lightly as he added, 'We must talk again later.'

On the surface it sounded a casual, friendly remark. But Elin knew differently. It was a statement of intent, almost a threat.

Her eyes that were jewel-bright and turbulent followed him as he left them, his lithe, confident walk serving to deepen her antagonism. Arrogance, power, and a virile strength she was instinctively afraid of were stamped into every line of him, and she took a quick sip of her drink to steady her jangling nerves.

At her elbow, James said, 'When I couldn't see you, I thought Garel must have beaten me to it, but since he hasn't how about coming outside to dance with me?'

She knocked back the rest of her Martini and, with a counterfeit smile, said, 'Why not?'

She was glad to take advantage of any excuse to get away from Garel Griffith's disturbing presence. Amid the crush he still commanded her attention, albeit against her will.

On moving away from her he had immediately been waylaid and was now the focus of an animated group. He looked dark and urbane, and his charm and aura of authority belonged to a man of position. It wasn't hard to see why people gravitated towards him. The pull of his attraction was powerful. Despising him didn't make Elin any the less aware of its strength.

She didn't mean to ask, because it was irrelevant to her whether or not he was lying, and yet, as she and James went out on to the patio, she heard herself say, 'Is Garel married?'

James drew her into the circle of his arms. 'No, not now,' he said. 'He's a widower.'

'A widower?' she echoed.

'Yes, his wife was killed in a car crash.' He shook his head slightly, as though he was speaking of the recent past. 'It was a dreadful tragedy.'

Elin absorbed the information in silence, glad of the music that meant she could allow the conversation to lapse. When later they returned to the drawing-room James had his arm lightly round her waist.

From across the room Garel's gaze drifted and caught hers. Something flickered in his eyes like a raw flame before someone walked in front of her, shielding her from him. Jarred, she knew she hadn't imagined the flaring of electricity in the air. The glance that had flown between them confirmed a potent and dangerous chemistry of attraction.

Thrown for an instant into total confusion, her mind raced to find some reason to give James for fleeing from the party. But the dusk was only just starting to deepen outside. She could think of no reason that wasn't going to sound hollow.

She took a quick steadying breath and pulled herself together. She wasn't a naïve twenty any longer, and no amount of sexual chemistry would ever make her weaken towards a man she hated. Besides, she had no intention of letting him know that she was single again. She was going to do her utmost to avoid him, but if he did corner her a second time she meant to parry both his questions and his subtle gibes with cold composure.

Several times in the course of the evening she felt the unsettling touch of his gaze. Mutinously she refused to let him suspect that he had in any way dampened her party mood. She recalled how he had reacted to meeting her again. As ever, he had been the complete master of the situation. His hardness and invincibility made her hate him all the more. Never was she going to let him guess the various ways she had paid for their one night together.

It was just before midnight when she decided she could leave the party without it looking as if she hadn't enjoyed herself.

'Must you go already?' James sounded both surprised and disappointed when she sought him out to say goodbye.

'What do you mean, already?' she said, an attractive thread of laughter in her voice. 'It's almost midnight. And anyway, I've got to phone for a taxi yet.'

'Why's that?' he asked, his warm eyes quizzical. 'I thought you'd come by car.'

'No, it's in for repairs at the moment.'

She deliberately skipped the details, knowing that if she mentioned how her car had been rammed by a Volvo James would ask her about the accident and keep her talking. For the first time she couldn't locate Garel, and, concerned that he might be about to close in on her at any moment, she was all the more anxious to slip away.

'Well, there's still no need for you to phone for a taxi,' James said. 'If you stay until the party's over I'll drive you home myself.'

'That's sweet of you,' she said appreciatively, 'but the party looks set to go on till the early hours.'

'So?' he quipped, trying to persuade her.

'So I'm not a late owl,' she smiled, ending the discussion.

It wasn't until she had escaped from the drawing-room that she realised how stiflingly hot it was among the crush. Other people had evidently made the same discovery and so had chosen to congregate in the hall away from the main body of the party.

She squeezed past a loud group who, with a lot of joking and laughter, were arguing about the controversial play that had just opened in the West End. One of the men looked her up and down with obvious masculine interest. She ignored him, skirted on embracing couple, and went quickly into the study.

She pushed the door to behind her, reaction setting in almost the moment she was alone. Her head was throbbing and her breathing was quickened, as though she had reached safety only by the narrowest margin.

The closed door muffled the noise of the party, making the study seem like a refuge. Her hand shook imperceptibly as she swept her dark brown hair off her forehead. She had feigned gaiety non-stop for almost two hours, and she felt like a limp wreck.

She leaned against the door a moment longer. Then, rousing herself, she crossed the luxurious expanse of Chinese carpet and sat down in the leather wing-backed chair behind James's desk. She found the Yellow Pages directory in the top left-hand drawer.

Some vague sense of danger made her start to hurry. The sooner she was home beyond Garel's reach and with the ordeal of the evening behind her, the better. Marking the number she wanted with her index finger, she was about to stretch out her hand to the phone when the door opened.

She glanced up sharply and then froze as she saw Garel.

'What are you doing in here all alone?' he enquired, irony in his tone. 'Not hiding, surely?'

He strolled towards her, a predator's grace in his supple stride. Icy poise immediately descended over her manner to disguise the chaos inside her. With frost chilling her voice, she parried, 'Who would I want to hide from? You?'

'It crossed my mind,' he agreed. 'You've certainly seemed very anxious to avoid me all evening.'

'If that were true I'd have left the party when you arrived,' she pointed out. 'The only reason I came in here was to phone for a taxi. I'm leaving now.'

He perched casually on the desk alongside her, his well-cut black trousers outlining the hard muscles of his thighs. Vitally male, he was too big and too close, and her heart began to thud unevenly.

'I'll give you a lift,' he offered.

'Not after last time,' she flashed back, and then deeply regretted the words.

Garel's dark eyes held knowledge and her skin burned even before he asked with lazy derision, 'Are you suggesting history might repeat itself?'

For one instant she thought her temper would snap, the next she had herself in check. The blaze of anger in her eyes died, her taut expression melting away as though it had been nothing more than a trick of the light.

'Ever the optimist, I see,' she quipped cynically.

She reached out and picked up the receiver, only to release it hastily as his fingers touched hers. Taking the receiver from her, he replaced it on its cradle.

'I told you I wanted to ring for a taxi,' she protested, irritation beginning to show in her voice.

'Are you afraid to be alone with me for some reason?' he asked sarcastically.

'Not in the least!' she snapped.

'Then why are you making such an issue about accepting a lift home?'

'I'm not!'

'Good. In which case, let's go.'

With a surge of annoyance she realised that she could only refuse at the cost of letting him see that her cool indifference to him was a sham. Hunching her shoulders as though it wasn't worth arguing over any longer, she gave in.

'All right,' she agreed. 'I'll get my jacket.'

It took her a minute or two to find it among the other short coats and wraps that had been left in the front bedroom. Stylish fitted cupboards with a large mirror above the dressing-table lined the far wall. As she slipped on her black bolero jacket she caught sight of her reflection.

Her taffeta dress looked crisp and uncreased. Her make-up was light and was as flawless as if it had just been applied. Her hair streamed smoothly down her shoulders. It reassured her to know that this was the cool, contained image she presented, whatever the vulnerability underneath. Feeling more of a match for Garel, she went downstairs.

He was standing in the hall talking to a dark-haired lovely who was wearing a simple sheath dress that was cut to within a hair's breadth of indecency. She had spent most of the evening with him, and they obviously knew each other well. Stormily Elin wondered how well.

As she watched he smiled at something the woman said. His smile was knowing, and all the more infuriating for being so attractive. Gritting her teeth against the smouldering anger she had been fighting to contain all evening, Elin continued down the stairs.

And then her gaze flew to the front door. If she was quick, she realised, she could cross the noisy hall and slip out into the street without Garel's seeing her go. Some chatting guests blocked her path. She skirted them swiftly and reached the front door. With the babel of voices and the throb of the music, the sound of it closing behind her was an inaudible click.

# CHAPTER TWO

WITH a sense of victory at having eluded Garel so neatly, Elin crossed the street that was lined with parked cars and began to walk away from the house. The warm soft night wrapped around her, the music which carried from the party giving way to the drone of traffic. In the distance she could hear the warning rumble of summer thunder. She never liked walking alone after dark, and she was glad she hadn't far to go to reach Baker Street station.

She had turned on to the main road with its bright street-lamps when she heard the ring of a man's measured footsteps following her. Her fingers tightened on her clutch-bag as she continued without turning, quickening her pace. Her feet began to race each other as the menacing steps rapidly closed the distance between her and whoever was behind her.

She was already on the side of the road she wanted for the Tube station. But, conscious that her pursuer was almost on top of her, she veered suddenly towards the kerb. Quickly she judged the speed of the oncoming car by its approaching headlamps, and would have crossed the road in front of it had the man not called her name at that moment.

She pivoted and took a step back. And then the fear went out of her eyes as she saw who it was who had been following her.

'You,' she gasped shakenly.

Garel's dark brows came together. He said brusquely, 'Did I frighten you?'

Only an instant ago she had been unutterably relieved to discover that she wasn't being tailed by some sinister stranger. Now, meeting Garel's gaze, and conscious with every inch of her of his swarthy attractiveness, her hostility towards him returned with a rush. Angry with herself for letting him see she'd been scared, she demanded, 'Wasn't that your intention?'

'I'm not some kind of pervert who goes about frightening women,' he fired back.

'Then you should know better than to walk tight on a woman's heels late at night.'

'I offered you a lift, remember?' he said with a touch of sarcasm. 'If you're really so nervous about being out alone after dark, why did you change your mind about accepting it?'

'You were standing talking to someone when I came downstairs. I didn't want to drag you away.'

'Or were you running away from me?'

'Why should I want to do that?' she asked coldly.

'I've no idea.' Taking hold of her by the arm, he went on casually, 'But my car's parked in the next side-street.'

His grip was firm and she resisted the impulse to struggle because it would be undignified. It aggravated her to be coerced, but what was equally maddening was to find that part of her was actually grateful to have the protection of his company now that it was late and lonely. Even so, she said, 'I appreciate your chivalry, but I'm only walking as far as the station. It's a good part of London. I'm not going to come to any harm, and I don't want to take you out of your way.'

'You're not taking me out of my way. Pinner's en route to where I live.' She slanted him a puzzled glance and he enlightened her, 'James told me.'

'What else——?' she began and then, cursing herself for being so transparent, broke off abruptly.

'What else did he tell me about you?' Garel enquired, guessing the rest of her question. 'Why? What dark secret are you hiding that you don't want me to know about?'

'I don't have any dark secrets.'

'Then there's no need to be defensive,' he said with deft irony as he guided her to where his Jaguar was parked under a street-lamp.

She waited till he had got in alongside her and then said, 'Exactly what's given you the impression that I am?'

'Perhaps the guarded looks you keep giving me,' he suggested, starting the ignition.

The interior light had gone off and his charismatic voice came to her from out of a dimness that was made more intimate by the green glow of the dashboard. She forced herself to sound amused.

'That's your imagination.'

The look Garel flickered at her was lightly sceptical. Although the Jaguar was roomy, she still felt much too closely confined with him. It cramped her efforts to appear relaxed.

He turned on to the main road and then asked casually, 'Has your husband moved jobs that you're living in London now?'

'Roger got the offer of a research post as soon as he completed his doctorate,' she told him evasively.

Her own coolness surprised her. She had been afraid

that, because his question had quickened her heartbeat, there would be a brittle note in her voice.

'I suppose he's using the car tonight,' Garel commented.

'It's a nuisance that mine's off the road at the moment,' she said, letting him think that his assumption was correct and anxious to get the topic off her ex-husband before she had to come up with some inventive lies instead of merely being economical with the truth. 'I was in an accident going to work last week. All the back of my car's stoved in.'

'Can you use the train to get to work?' he asked. 'Or is Roger able to drop you off?'

'He doesn't need to,' she replied. 'I work locally.'

'Doing what? When I knew you before, you were a student.'

She curbed the impulse to retort bitterly that when he'd known her before she'd been a fool. Instead she said, matching his conversational tone, 'I run a boutique. What about you? What are you doing these days?'

'I'm still in management consultancy, but I've formed my own company now,' he answered. 'So if ever you want any advice, or perhaps guidance about expansion at some date in the future, just give me a ring.'

She made the mental note that she'd see her business go bankrupt first, and thought from the glance he slanted her that he'd guessed it. Irritated, she turned her head away.

The silence lengthened, magnified by the low purr of the engine. She disliked the electricity and unrest she seemed to sense in the warm, shadow-drenched night. It was as if the quietness of the dark streets they drove along emphasised by contrast the static between them, and, meaning to break the undertow of tension, she said, 'I wonder if we'll get a storm tonight.'

'Are you finding it oppressive?'

The atmosphere was too charged for her to miss the double meaning in his question. Her skin felt suddenly hot, but, keeping carelessness in her voice, she answered as though she'd failed to catch any hidden implication.

'A bit.'

The attractive line of his mouth curved into a cynical smile and her eyes snapped. For the next ten minutes by the quartz clock set into the dashboard neither of them spoke. She hadn't realised she was fingering the links of her heavy gold bracelet until his alert gaze picked up the nervous movement. Promptly she relaxed her hands and, as she did so, he said, 'Whereabouts in Pinner do you live?'

'In the village, near the church.'

'Sounds nice. Do you have a large garden?'

'No, not very,' she answered. 'A manageable one, secluded and big enough for me.'

She realised the slip she'd made as soon as she'd spoken, but luckily Garel misinterpreted her reply. He commented, 'I take it you're the gardener in the family, not your husband.'

'Roger doesn't get much time,' she answered plausibly, lacing her hands together more tightly in her lap.

'The two of you seem to live rather separate lives.'

'What makes you say that?' she asked, promptly querying his observation.

'Merely that your interests and your social life don't appear to dovetail very closely with your husband's,' he mocked.

'Perhaps they don't, but that's my affair.'

'I'm sorry. I didn't mean to hit a nerve.'

His gibe annoyed her all the more because she was determined not to let him see she was annoyed. Feigning indifference, she said casually, 'Since you didn't, there's no need to apologise.'

He didn't contradict her and allowed the conversation to move on. It was the glitter of amused contempt she saw in his dark eyes that said he didn't believe her.

The sloping high street that was dominated by the old Norman church was quiet and empty as the Jaguar purred up it. Not even a leaf stirred among the horse-chestnut trees that crowned the rise, but, despite the heaviness of the air and the rumble of thunder, the storm still didn't break.

Because the turning into her road was sharp, Elin always slowed down for it in good time. When Garel didn't slacken speed she broke off what she was saying to remind him, 'It's this turning on the right.'

'Were you afraid I was about to abduct you?' he mocked as he cornered easily.

'To be honest, I wouldn't put anything past you,' she said tartly.

'I think I could say roughly the same about you,' he returned, and, to her fury, she gave him the satisfaction of seeing her blush. 'Which number is your house?'

Keeping tight rein on her temper, she answered, 'Thirty-two, but you can drop me here if you like. It's wider near the neck of the road to turn the car.'

'I'm planning on going straight on anyway,' he said, 'so it makes no odds.'

He drew up opposite her double-fronted house that

was built in the thirties' style of architecture. Its pretty white gables glimmered in the street-light. Quickly Elin pressed the catch of her seatbelt and opened her door.

'Thank you for the lift,' she said, and wasn't sorry that her tone sounded more polite than sincere.

'My pleasure,' he answered smoothly as he got out with her, obviously intending to see her to the door.

He escorted her across the road, their shadows merging as they walked together up the short paved drive. She felt about as safe with him as she would have done with a buccaneer, and nervousness made her fumble in her bag as she searched for her keys.

She was glad of the friendly light in the porch which helped her find them, and, as she looked up, Garel read out the name of the house, Bryn Lys, as it stood out clearly in the rays from the lamp.

'You've lost your Welsh lilt, but I see you don't want to break off all connections with the land of your fathers,' he commented.

'I'm still very tied to Wales, although I live in London now.'

A neighbour who took his dog for a nightly run was walking past, his Alsatian pacing in front of him. He called out a quiet goodnight.

'Goodnight,' she returned, and in that moment's distraction Garel relieved her of her house key.

'Give me back my key!' she demanded.

He inserted it in the lock and stood back for her to enter. Then, following her inside, he complied with her request.

'That was very neatly done,' she said furiously, her green eyes ablaze. 'But now you can get out!'

'So you do still have a temper,' he observed, sardonic

dryness in his tone. 'I was beginning to wonder.'

He stood with the oak door behind him, threateningly male for all his urbanity, and far too much the master of the situation. Aware of some intangible danger in the undeclared enmity between them, Elin immediately smothered the fires of her anger.

'It's well past midnight,' she stated pointedly. 'And I wasn't planning on making coffee.'

'Tomorrow's Sunday. You can sleep in.'

He made the comment casually, but she knew he had no intention of leaving. To gain time she turned and put her bag down on the hall table. Her back was to him, and yet with every inch of her she was aware of his height and virility, of his shattering closeness and the sexual tension that pulsed uneasily in the night.

Her heart began to thud unevenly. She despised herself for it, but she simply didn't have the nerve to make a stand. Tautly she conceded, 'All right, I'll make coffee.' She turned back to him, her voice firmer as she went on, 'But then I want you to leave.'

'Worried about your reputation in the street?' he gibed.

'Surely you can understand that I'd rather you weren't here when Roger comes in,' she countered.

'I don't intend staying that long,' he reassured her, although his intonation was faintly mocking.

Reluctantly she led the way into the spacious lounge, conscious as she drew the curtains across the french windows that he was appraising the room. Pale walls set off the Max Hofler landscape that was hung over the fireplace. A deep beige carpet complemented the colour scheme, as did the lightly patterned slipcovers on the armchair and sofa. There was a Japanese-style flower arrangement on the centrally placed coffee-table, while her collection of china and glass added to the charm of the room.

'You have a lot of flair when it comes to decorating a place,' Garel said. 'I like the mood you've created in this room. It's cool and sophisticated, the perfect setting for you.'

'You forget, design is my business,' she replied. She didn't want him to compliment her, if that was what his comment was.

She turned and went into the hall, pausing to slip off her jacket. Her kitchen faced south and greeted her with its usual warmth, but heavier tonight with the thundery weather. Sam, her cat, was curled up asleep on one of the chairs.

The thunder seemed to have moved away, and the hum of the refrigerator emphasised the stillness. Normally she liked the quiet solitude of the late hours with the rest of the world shut out, but now, with Garel waiting for her to join him in the lounge, the aura of intimacy it created unsettled her.

She made the coffee, accidentally pouring too much of it into the first cup. It spilt over, betraying her nervousness, and, irritated with herself, she fetched a cloth.

When she brought in the tray Garel was standing by the china cabinet looking at its contents. She knew he couldn't have missed seeing the cut-glass bowl he had given her and, as she set the tray down on the coffee-table, she said, 'I never thanked you for you wedding present.'

He glanced at her, a sardonic flicker in his dark eyes.

'I never expected you to,' he answered as he came to sit down in one of the armchairs.

'Then you must have been very sure I'd know the

reason why you chose it,' she said, a note of challenge in her voice.

'So sure, I'm surprised you kept it,' he said as he stirred his coffee.

She took her cup and sat down opposite him on the sofa.

'Perhaps,' she answered, 'I wanted to prove that, unlike the cut-glass bowl in Scott Fitzgerald's story, your gift of enmity couldn't put a curse on everything I care about.'

His mouth quirked with derisive humour. 'You read too much into it,' he told her. 'I'm not that malevolent.'

'You mean you merely intended it as a comment on my character?'

'Yes,' he agreed, and then went on, his compelling Welsh voice adding to the spell of the words, 'I wanted the present I gave you to be as hard as you are . . . and as beautiful——'

'I know the quote,' she interrupted frostily. 'And I'm still just as hard.'

His gaze ran over her, touching her long dark hair, the smooth curve of her bare shoulders, and her elegant legs that did justice to her short taffeta skirt.

'And just as beautiful,' he said.

'But *not* "as easy to see through",' she finished the quote.

He looked at her musingly.

'I wonder,' he murmured. Then as the door opened and her ginger and white tom came walking on silent paws into the room he said, 'I see you have a cat.'

The atmosphere of tension seemed to ease marginally and, glad of it, she answered, 'I found him one day skulking in the yard behind the boutique.'

'He's very handsome for a stray.'

'Yes, he is, though he wasn't when I first started feeding him.' Determined to give the impression of cool composure, she went on, 'His fur was dull and scruffy. He was very thin and terribly wary. It took a lot of coaxing before I could entice him into the boutique, and even longer before I dared pick him up.'

'Perhaps he'd been badly treated at some time,' Garel suggested as the cat advanced towards his outstretched hand. 'If so, he's obviously forgotten it now.'

'I don't think a cat ever forgets ill-treatment,' she said, her voice curiously expressionless, 'any more than a person does.'

'What's his name?' Garel asked as the cat nudged his hand and started to purr.

'Sam,' she answered, setting her cup aside and getting to her feet.

She skirted the coffee-table and scooped the large fluffy cat up into her arms. Scratching his head fondly, she cradled him to her as she returned to the sofa.

'He'll leave white hairs all over your suit if I let him get up on your lap,' she explained.

'I thought perhaps you didn't want him making friendly overtures to the enemy.'

There was an element of truth in his mocking remark, but she parried, 'Now *you're* reading too much into things.'

The cat settled down comfortably on her knee. The image she conveyed as she stroked him gave no indication that she was disturbed by Garel's masculine presence. The reality was different.

She disliked the way his long legs staked out a claim on the carpet. Tall, broad-shouldered and impeccably dressed, he made the lounge seem to shrink in size.

'How's your father keeping?' he enquired with a change of topic.

'He's very well,' she answered, wondering how much longer her nerves could stand this polite charade. 'And the mill, thanks to your consultancy advice, is going from strength to strength. Getting it listed as a tourist attraction was a great success.'

'I'm surprised you didn't decide to work in the business.'

'I told you, Roger's job came first.'

'Quite the dutiful wife, despite everything.'

She flashed him an angry look, knowing full well what he meant, and then just as quickly she curbed her temper. In a few more minutes he would be gone and she would be left with the satisfaction of knowing that, whatever the provocation, she had not lost her cool with him.

'Yes, I suppose I am,' she murmured.

She stretched out her hand to pick up her coffee-cup, hampered by the drowsy cat on her lap.

'You'll disturb Sam,' Garel said, getting to his feet to pass her cup to her so that she didn't have to move.

She took it from him, careful not to let her hand touch his. The pulse that beat at the base of her throat was the only indication of how vulnerable and feminine she suddenly felt with him standing over her.

'Thank you.'

Instead of returning to his armchair, he sat down beside her on the sofa.

'When did you grow your hair?' he asked. 'You used to wear it in a bob.'

She took a sip of coffee, not looking at him, but feeling his eyes on her and aware of the scant distance between them.

'I've worn it long for some time,' she said, too conscious of his hard thigh alongside hers to sound completely natural. 'I prefer this style.'

'So do I,' he commented, an unfathomable inflexion in his voice as he flicked a strand back from her shoulder. 'Long, it's like polished silk with blue-black lights.'

The brush of his warm fingers on her naked shoulder sent a shiver through her.

'Don't touch me!' she flashed.

His eyes glittered at her reaction to his careless caress. All at once the air seemed dense with unresolved tension and sexual awareness. At the same moment there was a loud crash of thunder. She started so noticeably that her cup rattled in its saucer.

'Your nerves are bad, Elin,' he mocked with a husky laugh.

She set her cup down with a slight clatter. Defending herself, she said, a brittle note in her voice, 'I hate a storm.'

'One often clears the air.'

Not sure if she was right to detect a hidden meaning in his remark, she didn't answer. A flash of lightning brightened the room as he asked unexpectedly, 'How long have you known James?'

She didn't know what he was getting at, and more than ever she didn't trust him.

'About a year.'

'What's your relationship with him?'

The crackle of thunder came again, almost like artillery fire. Tipping the sleepy cat off her lap, she stood up.

'He's my accountant,' she said coldly, nettled by his insinuation.

Garel also got to his feet. The sense of imminent and inescapable confrontation sent a flicker of panic through her. There was nothing hurried in Garel's movements, nothing to suggest that psychologically he was moving in on her all the time, yet she had to fight the impulse to take a couple of steps back.

'And is that *all* he is to you?' he asked sarcastically.

'I said, he's my accountant,' she repeated stonily, clenching her hands against her mounting anger.

Garel studied her a moment. A thin, mocking smile twitched the corners of his mouth for an instant.

'You'd like to order me to leave, wouldn't you, Elin?'

'At this moment, more than you could imagine!'

'Then it's time I gave you an excuse.'

His words warned her of his intention. She made to flee, only to be snatched hold of by the wrist and pulled hard against him. The sudden contact with his lean man's body momentarily took her breath away.

She saw the ruthless set of his jaw that was menacingly grim with purpose. Fury ran unchecked in her, and she thumped her fist against his shoulder.

'Don't you dare!' she gasped.

'So you've finally come back to being human, *cariad*,' he mocked, 'temper and all.'

She pushed at his arms as he bent his head. His hands that had snatched her captive had been brutal and, expecting his mouth to hold an equal savagery, she strained away to avoid its punishment.

Instead, the moment her lips opened under the determined force of his, he switched the kiss to one of expert mastery. She made a low, muffled sound of protest deep in her throat as she tried to fight the immediate hot stir of her blood. Struggling more furiously, she hit out at him again, turning her head away as she gasped, 'Let go of me!'

She caught a glimpse of his face, the arrestingly saturnine lines of it intensified, his eyes aglitter as he combed his fingers into her hair.

'When I'm ready,' he muttered harshly. 'Now try kissing me back.'

His fingers threaded more deeply into her dark hair as he found her mouth again. She couldn't escape from the arms that moulded her curves to fit the hard length of his male body. Her heart was pounding, embers of desire, long since forgotten, flaming under the persuasion of Garel's mouth. Hit by a helpless vertigo, for a crazy instant she wanted to slide her hands feverishly up around his neck.

And then out of the spinning confusion the past came rushing back. She wrenched herself free of his arms,

'How dare you!' she declared hoarsely. 'Now get out of here!'

He caught hold of her by the arm, his breathing as quickened as her own, and pulled her back to face him.

'I said, get out!' Her voice rose in a crescendo of anger.

'Why the change of heart?' he demanded, his words biting and sarcastic. 'Are you afraid your husband might walk in?'

'Yes!' she stormed. 'Afraid of his anger when he finds you here molesting me!'

He gave a short, humourless laugh.

'That's very good, Elin,' he returned, his mouth a wry line, before suddenly snatching up her left hand with swift violence, forcing her to look at her ringless finger. 'Except that you and Roger are now divorced!'

For a numbed moment she could only stare at him. Then, in a shaken, accusing voice, she began, 'You knew, didn't you? You knew all the time. That's why you came to James's party. I wondered why you didn't have a partner with you. I should have guessed it was because you intended cornering me.'

'Nicely deduced,' he agreed.

Furious with the way he had engineered their meeting and manipulated her, she went on, 'All those polite questions on the way home about Roger. You've been playing cat and mouse with me. Well, all right,' she flared, 'yes, I'm divorced. Now go ahead, sneer and say you're not surprised.'

Garel's dark eyes were unfathomable as he studied her. 'Tell me, what did Roger divorce you for, *cariad*?' he asked. 'Adultery?'

She crimsoned at the insult. Her fingers itched to slap him, and she curled them tightly into her palms as she fought to control her fury. With an angry, incredulous laugh she said, 'You really are a bastard!'

'And what am I supposed to deduce from that comment?' he jeered. 'That you did cheat on your husband, or that you didn't?'

'I never once was unfaithful to my husband,' she said, shaking with rage. 'Never! Do you understand?'

'You mean a wedding-ring stopped you from erring when an engagement ring didn't.'

Her temper suddenly snapped. Before she could stop herself she raised her hand and slapped him resoundingly across the face.

Her eyes focused on the slowly reddening mark on his lean cheek and, horrified and expecting swift retaliation, she took a step backwards, not realising that what had happened had been entirely at Garel's instigation, that he had deliberately goaded her until her control had finally shattered.

He caught hold of her smartly, pulling her to his chest as though he intended shaking her, and she gave a tiny gasp.

'The cool charade was very entertaining,' he rasped. 'But now it's over and I mean to have some answers from you.'

'Go to hell!' she said wildly, the thunder that crashed again adding to the fear that gripped her.

His eyes narrowed to piercing flintiness as he towered over her, dark and cynical and powerfully male.

'According to James you've been divorced for two years,' he said, demanding harshly, 'So why all the elaborate pretence? Why didn't you want me to know about it?'

'Because I knew how delighted you'd be!' she flashed back.

'Or was it because you felt you needed the protection of a non-existent husband?' he jeered as he released her.

'I . . . I don't know what you're talking about.'

'Don't you?'

She pivoted away from him, struggling to collect herself now that the flashpoint of their confrontation was over. With her back to him she said, 'Perhaps I did feel safer pretending I was still married to Roger.' Turning to face him again, she went on, 'But then, alone with a marauder like you, that's hardly surprising!'

'You have a very quaint turn of phrase at times.'

'A very apt turn of phrase,' she retaliated. 'Now, are you satisfied with the answers you've dragged out of me?'

'I will be when you've told me the reason why

you're divorced.'

Bitterly resentful of his interrogation, she snapped sarcastically, 'Why don't you ask James? He's been a most reliable source of information for you up to now.'

'I didn't grill him, if that's what you're implying. James is in love with you. He doesn't need any prompting to make you the main topic of conversation.'

Elin's lips parted slightly, a look of surprise replacing the anger in her eyes.

'You mean you didn't know?' Garel mocked.

'I don't believe you.'

'You're so blind you make me think perhaps James is right.'

'You're talking in riddles,' she said angrily. 'He's right about what?'

'That the reason why you're so reticent about your divorce is because you're still in love with your ex-husband.'

Her eyes darkened. She felt raw inside with the angry emotions he had unleashed in her.

'Why should you care one way or the other?' she demanded.

'Don't be stupid, Elin,' he fired back. 'You know damn well why I'm interested, just as you knew why I offered to see you home. You're the same wayward witch I knew five years ago, and I feel just the same about you as I did then. I want you.'

She stared at him. She saw the way his gleaming hair fell carelessly on to his swarthy forehead, the aggressive thrust of his jaw, his stern nose with the expressively flared nostrils. His mouth was hard and in his face there was a ruthless air of purpose.

'Are you propositioning me?' she said in a low,

furious voice.

He laughed.

'What a touching display of outraged virtue.'

She would have slapped him again had she dared.

'Get out!' she hissed.

His chiselled expression revealed very little except for the glitter of satisfaction in his eyes.

'Yes, I'll get out of your house,' he said. 'But don't expect me to get out of your life, because I'm no longer convinced that what was between us is over.'

With the warning delivered he turned and strode from the room. There was the sound of the front door as it closed behind him and then the roar of the Jaguar engine. It was followed by a crash of thunder almost overhead. A few minutes later came the clamour of heavy rain as the deluge started.

# CHAPTER THREE

WHEN the morning came the air was fresh after the rain and Elin drew back the curtains to see the sky tinged with blue. She had slept fitfully, unable to get Garel out of her mind, unable to stop reliving the events of that summer five years ago that had led, though Garel didn't know it, to her breaking off her engagement to the man she was finally to marry.

It had started off as such a happy summer. Roger had arranged to drive her home to Glasfryn in North Wales at the end of the term. In the two years she had been studying fashion and design she had grown to like the pace and bustle of London, but always, after a spell away, the grandeur and wild beauty of the mountain landscape struck her afresh.

Impulsively she had asked Roger to pull into the small lay-by when they reached the head of the pass so that she could get out for a few minutes and admire the view. Away from the road the terrain sloped steeply to a high, deeply incised valley before it rose again to distant craggy summits. The sun had been warm, and the peaceful stillness broken only by the sound of a rushing stream tumbling over its rocky course.

Roger had joined her, stretching his cramped shoulders before putting an arm around her.

'Are you tired?' she asked, looking up at him with a smile. 'If you want I'll drive the last bit of the way.'

'No, I'm fine,' he answered. 'Aren't the mountains

beautiful?'

'So beautiful, sometimes I wonder how I ever manage to go away and leave them.'

He turned her to face him, linking his arms lightly round her slim waist.

'I hope when we're married and have to live in Oxford you're not going to suffer from *hiraeth*,' he teased.

'I could be anywhere in the world and not be homesick as long as I'm with you.'

'Just the answer I wanted to hear,' he said lightly, and her soft laughter was lost as he claimed her mouth and kissed her.

With her engagement ring newly on her finger, it had seemed then as if nothing and no one could ever come between them. To her, Roger Llewellyn had possessed everything a girl could possibly want in a husband. He had looks, charm and a clever mind, which meant that at twenty-four he was all set for a prestigious career in the academic world.

Her father thought highly of him and liked his family, who were well off, and also in business locally. Though Elin hadn't seen it at the time, both families had done all they could to promote and encourage the romance. She had simply been pleased to know that her father, whom she loved very much, approved so whole-heartedly of the man she was marrying.

Because he needed the university facilities at Oxford in order to work on his thesis, Roger had been unable to spend as much time with her that summer as she'd have liked. But she understood that he was at a crucial stage with his research. She enjoyed those weekends when they managed to be together, while for the rest of her holiday she kept busy helping out in the design-room at the mill.

She liked the friendly atmosphere there and the feeling of tradition. The Glasfryn Woollen Mill had been in her family for almost a hundred years and, although her father didn't say as much, she knew he hoped that one day he'd have a grandson who would take over the running of it when he retired.

It had been towards the end of August when she had met Garel. Engrossed in checking a production pattern at the far end of the busy design-room, she hadn't immediately been aware of the man her father was showing around. She had looked up abstractedly to have her gaze collide with a pair of dark eyes that even at a distance stopped hers and held them with a sudden flash of masculine interest.

For an instant she felt almost lost, disturbed by the compelling impact of his gaze, yet completely unable to look away. And then the man turned to acknowledge an introduction to one of the members of the design team, and she was left staring at the back of his dark head and the strong line of his shoulders. He had the stance of a man used to coming on to the scene to set things straight, and, shaken by her reaction to him, she realised he must be the management consultant her father had called in to advise on the mill's expansion.

She had continued with her work, though her thoughts were so chaotic she scarcely knew what she was doing. She had never reacted that way before, never had her gaze inadvertently clash with a man's to find that her heart was racing.

Afraid to glance in his direction again, she kept her head lowered. Yet, even without the hubbub of conversation around her to alert her of the man's approach, she would have sensed that, accompanied by her father, he was heading in her direction.

She looked up as he stopped at her desk, sweeping her hair off her forehead with her left hand. The sunlight caught her solitaire engagement ring, making it flash with sudden brilliance, and she saw the man's astute eyes flicker to it as her father said, 'Mr Griffith, I'd like you to meet my daughter, Elin.'

At close range she judged him to be about thirty. Compared to her fiancé he wasn't a handsome man. His features were too ruggedly chiselled. Yet his masculine virility made him compellingly attractive.

His hair wasn't brown and wavy like Roger's, but was thick, straight and almost jet-black. His nose was straight, his mouth sensual, yet stern. But it was his eyes that held her arrested, just as they had done from across the room. They were a flinty brown, and behind them she sensed a mind as sharp as a precision tool.

She held out her hand as they exchanged hellos, all the more determined to appear collected because he made her feel so uncharacteristically flustered. His handshake was firm and hard and, though it wasn't challenging, it sent a flicker of electricity through her.

When he released her from his warm grasp her fingers still tingled, and she flexed them surreptitiously to dispel the disturbing sensation. He noticed and raised a speculative dark brow, querying her action.

Caught out, she coloured slightly and said, 'You have a firm handshake.'

'So I've been told,' he returned.

His voice was deep and resolute, and the inflexion in it told her that he was every bit as aware of the incomprehensible vibrations between them as she was.

The following evening her father invited him to

dinner. At first the conversation had centred on business and she hadn't taken a very active part in it. But under Garel's subtle guidance it soon moved on to topics of more general interest. He tried to draw her out, but she was too unsettled by his magnetism to drop her guard with him.

The were finishing dessert when the telephone started to ring.

'That will be Roger, I expect,' she announced. 'Will you excuse me?'

The conversation went on between Garel and her father as she left the room, but she felt the stab of his gaze between her shoulder-blades as she went out. It sent a strange little shiver down her spine.

But the call wasn't for her it was for her father. She resumed her place at the table, feeling ridiculously tongue-tied now that she and Garel were alone together. He came across so much as a man of the world. She was sure he must find her *ingénue*, perhaps even provincial.

'Is Roger your fiancé?' he asked.

'Yes,' she confirmed.

His eyes were very serious as he looked at her and she was conscious of a nervous quickening of her pulse. Usually she was good at making social small talk, but now she felt confused and self-conscious and, out of a sort of desperation, she said, 'Won't you have some more pie?'

'You're tempting me,' he answered. She was unprepared for the extra attractiveness his smile gave to his strong-featured face. 'You know, yours is the best apple and damson pie I've tasted since I was a kid and enjoyed my mother's cooking.'

'You don't enjoy it now?' she queried.

Immediately she realised how gauche and ridiculous she sounded, and flushed with embarrassment.

'Both my parents died when I was a child,' he answered. 'My aunt, who brought me up, was a dear soul, and I was very fond of her, but her best friend couldn't have said that she could cook.'

His remark took the edge off her unfortunate question, but though she smiled she was still cross with herself. She was used to playing the part of hostess when her father entertained, so she had no idea why all her usual composure should suddenly have deserted her.

After Garel had left, her father, who was clearly pleased that the evening had gone so well, said musingly, 'Well, what do you think of Mr Griffith?'

'He's very charming and very . . . very sure of himself,' she said, still trying to decide what there was about him that made her feel so apprehensive in his company.

'He has reason to be,' her father replied. 'He's astute, dynamic and an expert in his field.'

'How long is he going to be working at the mill?'

'Just for the next fortnight.' Her father laughed. 'With the fees his company charge, that's about as long as I can afford to have him on the premises.'

In those two weeks she became accustomed to seeing Garel walking about at the mill. She would pass him on the stairs, or when she was crossing the yard, and always he would make a point of pausing to speak to her. She had no idea that the restlessness that began to take hold of her at the end of that summer had more to do with him than with the fact that her fiancé seemed to forget her existence when he was immersed in his research.

If Roger hadn't let her down that last weekend of the holiday, the Friday evening Garel had spent discussing the mill's expansion with her father might have marked the end of their acquaintance. Disappointed that Roger had cancelled their plans, she had accepted a last-minute invitation to go out for a drink with a group of friends.

She could hear voices coming from the study as she returned home and, as she took off her jacket, the door to it opened and her father and Garel came into the hall. He stood, tall, dark and powerful in a charcoal-grey suit that seemed to emphasise the lean strength of his body.

'Hello, Elin,' he said, his deep voice seeming to put poetry into her name as his gaze held hers.

'Hello.' For some reason her heartbeat had quickened. It made her sound a mite breathless, and she coloured as she saw his faintly amused smile.

'Did you have a good evening?'

'Yes, thanks, Dad.'

'Pity Roger couldn't be here to enjoy it with you.'

She felt Garel's eyes on her and knew with a flicker of irritation that he was wondering exactly what sort of relationship she and her fiancé had when they always seemed to be apart. Though she addressed the comment to her father, it was for Garel's benefit that she said, 'His work has to come first, especially now that he's so close to completing his thesis.'

'I understand your new term starts on Monday,' Garel stated conversationally. 'As I'm going back to London tomorrow, can I offer you a lift?'

'That's most kind of you,' her father interposed. 'Elin was thinking she'd have to get the train.'

The arrangement had been made without her even

having spoken.

For the first few miles of the journey the conversation between them was spasmodic. It wasn't until they were speeding through the beautiful rolling countryside of Shropshire that Elin began to relax with him. The curious tension she had sensed between them since their first meeting disappeared as deliberately Garel put her at her ease, amusing her and making her laugh.

They stopped for lunch at Broadway. The honey-coloured stone buildings glowed in the bright afternoon sunshine and, although the summer was drawing to a close, tourists still sauntered along the tranquil main street and milled around the numerous antique shops.

They went into one and browsed among the assortment of books. It turned out that their tastes were very similar when it came to reading. Crouching down to examine the titles on the lowest shelf of a bookcase that was wedged between a military chest and a walnut table, she discovered a copy of Scott Fitzgerald's short stories.

She straightened up with the book in her hand and, as she did so, her arm nudged his, making her stumble. He caught hold of her to steady her. For an instant her pulse leapt nervously at his touch and she was unable to camouflage her shattering awareness of him.

'I . . . I'm sorry,' she stammered. 'I'm being clumsy.'

'You couldn't be clumsy if you tried. You're as graceful as you're beautiful,' he said, adding as he saw the effect his words were having on her, 'And you blush most prettily.'

His smile was unfairly attractive and she returned it

without thinking, cementing the rapport between them.

Taking the book from her, he glanced at the cover and commented, 'Fitzgerald. He's a favourite of mine. All his work has something to say, not just the well-known novels like *The Great Gatsby* and *The Beautiful and the Damned*, but his short stories too.'

'Do you think I should buy it?' she smiled.

'The collection's worth buying just for the first short story alone.'

It was entitled 'The Cut-Glass Bowl', and on his recommendation she went ahead and bought the book before they strolled back to the car. They didn't stop again except for petrol just before they picked up the motorway.

As they approached London, Garel glanced at her and said, 'Have dinner with me tonight.'

Taken unawares, she faltered, 'I don't think . . . '

'Why not?' he enquired.

'Well, because . . . '

'Because your fiancé's the jealous type and you're afraid he would object, or because you're not over fond of my company?'

'No, of course not,' she protested.

'Which question is that an answer to?'

'Roger doesn't get jealous for no reason and——' She broke off.

'And?'

'I . . . I don't dislike your company,' she confessed.

'Then where would you like to go this evening?' Garel asked.

She would probably have said that she'd leave the choice to him, had not the forcefulness of his personality made her feel the need to establish her own assertiveness. She knew that his home was in Denham and, picking somewhere that would be convenient for him, she suggested, 'How about one of the hotels near the airport?'

'Fine,' he agreed.

When they reached the small terraced house in Northolt, where she lived in term-time, he lifted her case out of the boot and carried it inside. The girl Elin shared with was still away and the house had a quiet, undisturbed feel to it.

Garel took her suitcase upstairs for her, and then, as she thanked him and saw him out, said, 'I'll call for you at eight.'

When he had gone she unpacked, trying the whole time to justify her acceptance of his invitation. Certainly, since he knew she had no plans for the evening, it would have been hard to find a tactful refusal. Besides, she was sure Roger wouldn't mind, so it was ridiculous to be feeling vaguely guilty. She had enjoyed the drive and the countryside had been beautiful. It would have somehow been an anticlimax to round the day off with an evening alone.

Catching sight of the time, she took a quick refreshing shower and then began to get ready. She slipped on a silk jade dress that showed up her eyes as pure emerald. The skirt fell most flatteringly, emphasising her slimness, while thin straps crossed lightly tanned shoulders. With it she wore sheer stockings and pretty high-heeled bronze sandals.

Her dark lashes looked longer than ever once she'd swept them with the mascara brush. She applied her make-up with a light hand and left her hair loose, determined not to go to any special trouble with her appearance for a man who was very charismatic, but who had no relevance in her life. Even so, though he made no spoken comment, his dark eyes when she opened the door to him were blatantly admiring.

The hotel he drove them to was busy, but a very deferential head waiter promptly showed them to one of the best tables. Before she turned her attention to the menu she glanced about. Silver and crystal gleamed on the white linen tablecloths, while huge vases massed with flowers were placed on console tables, adding to the charm of the setting.

Garel had told her briefly about his upbringing during the drive back from Glasfryn. He had said that it had been a struggle financially for him to go to university, but had he not mentioned it she would have assumed quite automatically from the attention he commanded from the waiters, and from his easy *savoir-faire*, that his background was every bit as moneyed as her own.

Reluctantly she admitted that he intrigued her. Particularly she found herself wondering about the romantic side of his life. He was attractive enough, she thought ruefully, to have a whole harem of women.

'You're very quiet suddenly.'

Garel's deep voice broke into her thoughts and she glanced up to find him watching her.

'I was thinking.'

'What about?'

'I was wondering if you make a practice of asking different women out to dinner.'

It was quite unintentional, but her remark sounded flirtatious. With an amused smile, Garel answered, 'Only when they're attractive and I happen to be spending the weekend alone.'

Her eyes laughed in reply. His masculine charm was

such that she couldn't help responding to it.

As they ate they talked easily. It surprised Elin that, despite their having spent all day in each other's company, there was still so much to talk about. Garel had broken down her defences completely, and everything she said seemed to interest him. The time flew past, the rapport between them so strong that, despite the other diners, the babel of voices and the tinkle of crockery, they might have been alone.

They lingered over coffee and liqueurs, and it was late when they finally left the restaurant. The night air was warm and sultry, adding to the wayward enchantment of the evening. From the airport perimeter road came the drone of traffic, and there was the thunderous roar of aircraft taking off for distant destinations. Landing lights flashed overhead in the darkness.

As Garel's car sped through the bright London streets she leaned her head back against the leather headrest.

'Tired?' he asked with a slight smile.

'A little,' she confessed contentedly. 'It's been such a lovely day.'

'It's been more than that,' he said quietly, a sensual quality to his charismatic Welsh voice. 'It's been a day to treasure.'

The glance that flew between them as he spoke was as intimate as a caress. There was something unequivocal about it and for a bewildering instant she felt no longer mistress of her own destiny. Hurriedly she dropped her gaze, her heartbeat quickening.

Once again there was static in the air, a sexual awareness that made the night enmeshed with dangerous possibilities. A hot little shiver traced over her skin and, deeply disturbed by the electricity between them, she made no attempt to answer.

The streets were virtually deserted and they were quickly back at her house. When his car drew to a halt, alarmed by the attraction he had for her, she already had her key in her hand. They had hardly spoken during the last part of the journey, but now he turned to her in the romantically shadowed darkness.

'Elin——' he began quietly.

Frightened that if she let herself listen to what he was about to say their relationship might ignite into something beyond her control, she interrupted nervously, 'It was very kind of you——'

She broke off abruptly, a concerned frown appearing between her brows as suddenly she noticed that there was a light shining through the drawn curtains at the front bedroom window of her house.

'What's wrong?' Garel asked with swift perceptiveness.

'There's a light on upstairs,' she answered. 'My flatmate's not coming back for the new term till tomorrow. I . . . I must have left it on by mistake.'

'Except that you don't think you did,' he summarised accurately. 'I'd better come in with you in case you've been burgled. Give me your key.'

She hoped desperately that the house hadn't been broken into while they'd been out, that she wasn't going to find utter chaos inside. Responding to the masculine authority in his voice, she quickly dropped her key into his outstretched palm.

He walked up the front path with her, unlocked the door and pushed it open. His left hand found the light switch while with his right he moved her firmly and protectively behind him, taking no chances with her safety when there was a possibility that the house might not be empty.

The hall was exactly as she'd left it.

'It all looks OK,' Garel said, but just the same he motioned her to stay where she was by the front door while he strode through the downstairs rooms. Returning to the hall, he went swiftly upstairs.

Elin's eyes flickered upwards to the ceiling as she heard him go into her bedroom. A moment later there was a sudden loud thud. Her heart skipped a beat with fear and she gasped aloud, 'Garel . . .?'

A pottery vase stood on the hall table and with desperate spirit she snatched it up. She had already rushed to the foot of the stairs by the time he called back, a note of humour in his voice, 'It's all right, Elin. I've just walked into your suitcase. You must have left the light on. There's . . .'

He appeared at the top of the staircase, pausing in his explanation as he saw her below him. She had collapsed with relief against the wall.

He continued down the stairs and then gently took the vase out of her hand.

'Were you coming to my defence with this?' he asked, teasing her almost tenderly as he replaced the vase on the hall table.

'Don't make fun of me,' she said with a shaky laugh. 'For a minute there I was really scared.'

'And I'm touched,' he murmured, grazing her cheek with one lightly caressing finger.

Her breath seemed suddenly to catch in her throat. Incapable of moving, she stood looking up at him, mesmerised by the dark intensity in his eyes, her heart hammering against her ribs.

'You're trembling,' he said softly.

They were standing only inches apart. She was conscious of his deep chest, of the breadth of his strong shoulders. The fragrance of his aftershave was crisp and intoxicatingly masculine.

She couldn't seem to drag her gaze away from his. It was as though she was in a trance and, acting on an impulse she was powerless to control, she reached her hand up to trace the hard, exciting line of his jaw. Immediately she was horrified by her provocative boldness.

She made to snatch her hand away, but Garel caught hold of it, pressing an ardent kiss into her palm. A violent shiver went through her.

'Garel . . .' she breathed, agonised by what was happening, though it had been inevitable from the moment they'd met.

'It's all right, *cariad*,' he murmured, moving nearer still so that their bodies touched as his hand caressed her cheek.

She could feel the hardness of his thighs against hers and her pulse quickened dizzily, making colour flame in her cheeks.

'No . . .' she whispered faintly, in the grip of emotions so powerful and so alien that she scarcely knew what she was saying.

But already it was too late. Garel bent his head slowly, enfolding her tightly, crushing her against the lean length of his man's body. His mouth as it found hers was like nothing she had ever felt before, tender, hungry and demanding, setting her on fire.

She moaned deep in her throat, her hands that had gone to repulse him tightening on his shoulders to steady herself as her lips parted helplessly under his. Nothing in her life had prepared her for the fierce tide of pleasure that ran like molten gold along her veins. His insistent kiss seemed to shake her to the very soul.

When finally his plundering exploration of her mouth stopped and he raised his head, she stared up at him with dazed, darkened eyes.

'Elin . . .' Garel's voice was low and ragged, his breathing as short and irregular as her own.

She scarcely heard him. The sudden wild flaring of sexual chemistry between them terrified her and, in a confused panic, she broke free from his arms and fled into the lounge. Her heart was beating so fast that she felt almost faint, and she clutched hold of the mantelpiece to steady herself.

Almost immediately Garel's hands were on her shoulders, his palms warm, firm and caressing. He turned her insistently towards him, his eyes glittering as he saw the rapid rise and fall of her breasts, the flush of desire on her face.

'Kiss me,' he demanded.

'Don't . . . I . . .' she whispered, hypnotised by the burning look in his eyes that was making her tremble in every nerve. 'Garel, please . . .' she pleaded. 'I . . . I can't think.'

'I don't want you to think,' he muttered huskily. 'I want you to touch me, to kiss me back.'

She shook her head imperceptibly, trying desperately to overcome the weakness that had taken hold of her.

'No——' she began, but the words were taken from her as his mouth touched hers.

Against her lips he murmured huskily, 'Don't fight it, Elin. You were mine from the moment we met. You know you were.'

# CHAPTER FOUR

THE ringing of the church bells that filled the Sunday morning with music broke into Elin's thoughts. With a slight start she came back to the present, her throat tight with tears she was determined not to shed.

She had just begun to get her life in order, so why, after five years, did her path have to cross Garel's again? If only, she thought bitterly, she hadn't gone to James's party last night. Then none of these violent emotions would be tearing at her now. She could have gone on forgetting.

And yet, deep down, she knew it was a self-delusion to think she could ever forget. What had happened between her and Garel would always be burned indelibly into her mind.

Despite her resolve to stop tormenting herself with the past, she thought back yet again to that morning five years ago, a morning so like this one with its sunshine and Sunday peacefulness. She had stirred drowsily, enveloped by a cathartic contentment. It had been an instant before she had realised that she was not alone in bed, that Garel's chest was pressed closely against her back, that his hard body was wrapped behind hers.

Then, like a thunderbolt, recollection had come rushing back. When she and Garel had become lovers it had not only seemed right and beautiful, it had seemed almost predestined.

Yet, waking beside him, she was swamped with a

sense of shock. She was engaged to Roger. She had gone out with him for over a year, cared for him enough to agree to marry him, so how was she now lying naked with Garel's arm thrown possessively across her waist?

Dazed by the loss of her virginity, she twisted to look at him, her mind a maelstrom of guilt and confusion. The sheet was twisted around his hips, and she could see the steady rise and fall of his deep chest with his even breathing. His hair was tousled, his strong-featured face relaxed and yet, even in sleep, retaining all of its forcefulness of character.

I love him, she thought, bewildered. The tumult inside her suddenly stilled as she recognised the truth. She not only loved Garel, but together they had found a perfect completeness. She remembered his passion, his urgency and his control as he had seduced her. She belonged to him just as he had said.

Her heart was filled with wonder and then Roger fell as a shadow across her thoughts. She hated the idea of hurting him, of telling him, as she must, that she had fallen in love with someone else. He had a lot of pride, and just the gossip alone that their broken engagement would cause in the small community of Glasfryn would be hard on him. She could imagine her father's disappointment in her, too.

Her happiness dimmed a little. She eased herself gently away from Garel and slid off the bed. She reached for her wrap, her gaze returning to him again while she drew it on. The glow of love, and the pleasure it gave her just to look at him, strong and sleeping, amazed her.

His jacket was on the floor where she had pushed it from his shoulders in her hungry need to caress him.

She stooped to pick it up and, as she did so, his wallet fell out and flopped open on to the carpet. Her heart jolted as she saw the photograph inside it.

Breathless, she sank down on her knees. The rest of the room receded as for a timeless frozen moment she stared at the close-up picture of a smiling woman and the dark-haired little boy. There could be no mistake. The resemblance between the child and the man she had just slept with was too striking. She was staring at a photograph of Garel's son and Garel's wife.

Sick and dizzy with dismay, she flipped the wallet shut, clenching it tightly in her hand as though she could press the secret it contained back between the leather cover. Voices from the previous evening echoed mockingly in her head, her own asking Garel if he made a practice of asking different women out to dinner, and then his, as he answered, 'Only when they're attractive and I happen to be spending the weekend alone.'

Anger and despair trembled through her. She felt shattered, destroyed, furious at her own naiveté. She had believed that Garel's possession of her had been a pledge of love. Instead she had been a one-night stand for a married man whose wife happened to be away that weekend.

A tear traced down her cheek and, adamant that she would not cry, she cut off the playback of memory, fighting to get hold of her emotions. What was wrong with her, that she had lain awake half the night over a man who was a womaniser and a liar? Garel had caused her enough misery.

But he wasn't going to cause her any more, she resolved, as she pulled herself together. She had found self-sufficiency, independence and a measure of happiness in the last two years, and no one, least of all a man she hated and despised, was going to wreck her calm, or distress her.

Normally after a busy week she enjoyed her Sundays, which were quiet and leisurely, but, more shaken by Garel's reappearance in her life than she would admit, she was glad when Monday came. She not only liked running her own business and the feeling of success it gave her, but work helped her to push all other problems into the background.

She was standing in one of the bow windows, finishing changing the display, when her assistant arrived. The opening of the door set the shop bell tinkling. She glanced up from where she was spreading out the skirt of a breezy silk dress and began, 'At last the summer's come, so I thought we'd entice the customers with some Ascot-style clothes.'

Miriam checked her watch and said in surprise, 'What time did you get here this morning?'

She had been awake at just after six, unable to sleep for the second night in succession. Having sat over breakfast with the newspaper and completed most of the cryptic crossword, she had seen no point in lingering at home any longer. She said flippantly, 'Early.'

'It must have been,' Miriam laughed. 'Anyway, as long as I'm not late.'

She bustled into the workroom at the back of the boutique to hang up her jacket. Cheerful, energetic and capable, she had worked at the shop for just over a year. Leaving the door ajar, she called out chattily, 'Wasn't the thunder dreadful on Saturday night? Were you back from the party when we had that torrential rain?'

'Yes, luckily,' Elin said, adding as Miriam came out from the workroom, 'Would you fetch me the red Giavannozzi suit and the navy and white MaxMara dress? I'd like them for the other window.'

Miriam went over to the rail and commented as she drew out the garments Elin wanted, 'A wide-brimmed boater would be perfect with this suit. Have you thought of going in for a few hats? They're supposed to be making a come-back this year, and there's no milliner's in Pinner.'

'It's an idea, but we don't really have the space for them,' Elin said. 'And I'd rather stick to what we know will sell.'

'Perhaps you're right,' Miriam agreed. She handed Elin the Giavannozzi suit and then asked, 'Did you have a good weekend? How was the party?'

'It was all right.' Elin shrugged lightly, and then, because she needed to tell someone, she admitted, her tone betraying very little, 'I met an old flame.'

'How exciting! Tell me more. What's he like?'

'Oh, not much different from when I knew him before. A bit older, but then so am I.'

There was a wealth of subtle meaning behind her simple statement, but Miriam, failing to catch it, commented, 'Wouldn't it be nice if the two of you could rekindle the affair?'

Elin shook her head. 'Not a chance,' she said as she stabbed a pin into the jacket she was adjusting on the model.

'Why's that?' Miriam asked. 'Is he married?'

'No,' Elin said drily, and added mentally, *not now*.

'Well, then, the two of you could get together again.'

'Pass me a couple more pins, would you?' Elin

asked before saying firmly, 'I don't want to get involved, either with him or with anyone else.'

'Was your divorce very traumatic, that you're dead set against another relationship?'

Elin ran her hand through her hair. 'It . . . it wasn't the divorce that was traumatic,' she said. 'It was the marriage itself.'

'In what way?' Miriam asked, crinkling her brow. 'Did your husband drink or something?'

'He wasn't exactly what you'd call a drinker,' Elin said. 'He only got drunk once in a great while . . . but . . . but when he did we'd have these awful rows. I'd no idea he drank other than in a social way until after we were married, or that he had such a demon of a temper.' She kept the explanation brief and went on, 'What made it worse was that we were living abroad at the time. My husband got the offer of a research post at the University of B.C. in Vancouver soon after we were married.'

'So you had no one you could confide in,' Miriam guessed.

'Roger didn't want me to work, which meant that all my friends were really his friends. I couldn't talk to them about my marriage. And I didn't want to worry my father. When I wrote home I never mentioned that things weren't working out between Roger and me, and at first after the rows he was always so anxious to make up. It made me keep hoping that things would get better.'

'Which they didn't.'

Elin took a deep breath and shook her head. It was much too painful even to attempt to recount everything that had happened.

'When I finally realised that the marriage was over,'

she sighed, 'I swore I was going to put it all behind me. But somehow it's not so easy. However much you want to, you can't slam the door shut on the past. Some of it stays with you for always.'

There was a pause, and then Miriam said musingly, 'Maybe it's just as well we can't erase the past. If we could, we'd never learn from experience.'

'Which I certainly did,' Elin said wryly. 'Lesson number one being not to marry again.'

'But the next time you might be happy,' Miriam protested.

'It's not a risk I'd want to take,' Elin said. 'On my own I know where I stand. Falling in love with a man means laying yourself wide open to heartbreak. I'm determined never to go through that again.'

'You were just unlucky,' Miriam persisted. 'A lot of people who are divorced go on to make happy second marriages.'

'Perhaps, but I've no intention of marrying for a second time.'

'You can't mean that. Apart from anything else, surely you'd like to have children?'

Elin felt a pang of wistfulness. Ignoring it, she said as if she were quite positive, 'It sounds selfish, but freedom's more important to me.'

'It's a pity,' Miriam sighed. 'Some man would count himself really lucky to have you as his wife and the mother of his kids.'

'Are you after a rise, or just next Saturday off?' Elin joked.

'Neither,' Miriam laughed. 'All I want is for you to tell me that the old flame is tall, dark and handsome.'

Elin paused, and then conceded grudgingly, 'In a hard sort of a way I suppose you could say he's good-looking, but I'm still not interested. Now, let's unpack those blouses that were delivered on Saturday. A couple of them in white and navy would finish this window off nicely. And then I think we deserve a cup of coffee.'

'Good idea,' Miriam agreed, adding, 'By the way, Mrs Armstrong said she'd call in this morning. I've hung the skirt I've altered for her on the rail in the fitting-room.'

Miriam, who was a skilled dressmaker, undertook all the fitting work, leaving Elin with more time to devote her talents to the management of the business.

For a Monday they were fairly busy, and the morning flew. Although Elin had said very little about Garel, she felt better for having talked. It had helped put the events of Saturday night into some kind of perspective.

Despite his parting shot that things weren't yet over between them, on reflection she didn't really believe that Garel would contact her again. She had shown her contempt for him too clearly, and, in any case, when he had such a low opinion of her why should he want to?

But she was wrong. It was near to closing time on Thursday, and she was returning to the rail some dresses that a customer had discarded in favour of her final purchase, when he walked into the boutique. She glanced up with an enquiring smile that went cold as she saw his tall, lithe frame in the doorway.

Caught off guard, she demanded defensively, 'What are *you* doing here?'

'Do you make courtesy to the customer your top priority?' he mocked. 'I want to buy a thank-you present for someone.'

The static between them was such that it took no more than that simple exchange of words to set her heart thumping. His presence dominated the tranquil, very feminine surroundings, making the boutique seem smaller than it was. With an effort of will she mastered the impulse to retreat. Tilting her head to a regal angle, she said, 'I'd be very surprised if there's anything here that would take your eye. I don't stock lingerie or seductive nightgowns.'

'It's not *that* sort of thank-you present,' Garel corrected her, a gleam of sardonic amusement in his brown eyes. 'I want nothing more intimate than a scarf, a simple silk square, something tasteful.'

She strongly suspected that he had chosen to make the purchase at her boutique instead of going elsewhere purely to irritate her. Determined to deny him that satisfaction, she said coolly, 'I don't sell anything that isn't tasteful. If you'll wait here a moment I'll ask my assistant to come and serve you.'

Immediately his hand closed on her arm, detaining her. His grip was no more than firm, but she started at the live warmth of his touch like a nervous filly and, furious with herself, knew that her reaction hadn't escaped him.

'You spend a lot of time these days running away,' he said with light sarcasm. 'Why, I wonder? Whatever else you are, I wouldn't have thought you were a coward.'

The gibe hit home on several counts. Snatching her arm away from him, she snapped, 'You're detestable! I've never had the misfortune to meet anyone who was less of a gentleman!'

His mouth quirked mockingly as he answered, 'Well, now that we're even with exchanging insults, shall we call a truce so you can show me some scarves?'

His personality was too forceful for her to be misled into thinking he was putting forward a suggestion. He was issuing her with an order. Much as it went against the grain to swallow her anger, she preferred to take refuge behind a wall of distant politeness than to risk another clash with him of the sort that had developed between them on the night of James's party.

'Very well,' she said coolly. 'Since the rule of good business is never to lose a sale, we'll call a truce.'

'Always so practical,' he sad lazily.

She had a hunch that what he meant was that she was hard, but she didn't dignify his comment by challenging it. Instead she went behind the counter and, bowing her head, opened one of the shallow drawers beneath it.

Aware of Garel's unsettling masculine gaze on her, she selected half a dozen scarves in various Paisley patterns and spread them out for him to look at on the glass-topped counter.

'Was this the sort of thing you had in mind?' she enquired.

He paused a moment, and then said, 'No. They're pretty enough, but I'd like something rather more original in design. These are too safe.'

She refolded them, speculating stormily on who the woman was he was buying the present for. Not wanting him to read her thoughts, she quickly veiled her green eyes with her lashes and murmured, 'We have a wide selection of scarves, Gucci, Hermés, Jacqmar, all the best houses. I'll show you some that are a little more off beat.'

He considered the silk squares she spread out for

him with a judicial air, taking his time. With his attention diverted, she paused in her sales talk and allowed herself to study him.

The strong lines of his face were aggressively masculine. His brows were thick and dark. Tiny lines were etched at the corners of his eyes, but it was too long since they had laughed together for her to acknowledge that he possessed a quick sense of humour. His mouth was firm with a touch of ruthlessness to it.

She remembered its plundering mastery when he had kissed her on Saturday, and her pulse quickened with anger and another emotion she refused to name. She would not accept that she could be in any way physically attracted to a man she hated.

Hurriedly, while the conviction still held, she glanced away from his mouth and looked at his hands as he picked up one of the silk squares. They were long and expressive. He handled the scarf as though appreciative of the quality of the fabric.

'This one's very attractive,' he announced. 'Would you mind tying it round your neck so I can get the effect?'

Her thoughts of an instant ago were too disturbing for her to be able to meet the directness of his hawkish eyes.

'Not at all,' she murmured coolly.

She folded the scarf, knotting it casually so that the ends fell wispily over the front of her coffee-coloured blouse.

Garel tilted his head to one side as he appraised her. His dark eyes moved leisurely from the perfection of her features to her slender neck, travelling down to the hollow of her throat. His masculine gaze was a deliberate reminder that not one line of her hidden body was unknown to him, and a becoming tinge of angry colour spread along her cheekbones.

Her outrage was obvious, and a satisfied glint flickered in the depths of his eyes, as though he had raked her with his gaze with the express purpose of getting a rise out of her. Yet his voice was bland as he commented about the scarf, 'It's very stylish. And it looks well on you. But I don't know that it's right for the person I'm buying it for.'

'You could always try another shop!' she retorted.

Satirical amusement carved faint grooves in his lean cheeks and she had the strong desire to slap him.

'I'm sure that won't be necessary,' he said with deft irony. 'You said you stocked a wide selection of scarves.'

'Then, since you seem to have such a clear idea of what you want, perhaps you could describe it for me so that I don't have to get the whole shop out for you!'

'I thought that was what you were prepared to do if the customer required it,' he mocked.

Breathing in deeply, she checked the flow of her temper. He was needling her in much the same way as he had done on the night of James's party, except that there was less malice in it for some reason.

Giving him an entirely manufactured smile, she said, 'Not many customers are that difficult. Is there any colour you wanted especially?'

The groove deepened around his mouth.

'I was thinking of mauve, or maybe blue, the sort of colour that will complement auburn hair, and eyes the colour of wild irises.'

'How very poetic!' she said with light derision.

'I was wrong when I said you'd lost your attractive

lilt,' he remarked lazily. 'You still get it back in your voice at times.'

It was perfectly true. When her temper was up the rhythm in her voice was discernible as Welsh. Irritation flashed through her at his damnable perceptiveness.

With great restraint she ignored his gibe and came round the counter to walk over to a display cabinet. The boutique was well carpeted and Garel's almost silent tread as he joined her put her in mind of a stalking predator. Her nerves tightened, and in a cool voice she asked, 'Do you see anything here that you like?'

'Yes, that one folded at the back looks interesting.'

She opened the cabinet and went to unpin a geometrically patterned scarf in various shades of blue.

'No, not that one,' he corrected her. 'The one to your right.'

It was printed in an artistic swirl of cobalt and amethyst colours. She took it out of the cabinet and draped it over her hand for him to look at. She was sure he was being deliberately hard to please, and was fully expecting him to make her dismantle the entire display. Having steeled herself not to demur, she was surprised when he said, 'That's perfect. It's exactly what I'm looking for. I'll take it.'

Calmly she read out the price-tag to him. It was nothing to her if he chose to shower his latest mistress with expensive presents, and yet her eyes were turbulent as she slipped the scarf into a gold gift envelope.

Garel wrote out a cheque and handed it to her together with his cheque-card. She passed the cheque-card back to him with a cool, 'That won't be necessary. I'm sure I can trust you where money's concerned.'

He slanted a quizzical dark eyebrow at her.

'And what does that veiled statement hide?' he enquired.

The fuse to her temper had been burning from the moment he had stepped into the boutique, and she was just about ready to give in to the temptation to match words with him. It was the vague comprehension that possibly that was precisely what he wanted which stopped her.

Miriam came out of the fitting-room and, taking advantage of the diversion to avoid answering him, Elin said, 'I hadn't realised it was so late. I'll lock up, Miriam, when I've finished serving this customer, so it's all right for you to go. Just put "Closed" on the door as you leave.'

As her assistant went out into the street, Elin handed Garel his receipt and remarked, 'It's a beautiful scarf. I'm sure the person you've bought it for will enjoy wearing it.'

'Your sales patter's very good,' he returned sarcastically, 'but you don't evade the question so easily. I asked you what you meant by your oblique comment.'

'What oblique comment?' she asked, feigning blankness, her heartbeat beginning to quicken with the tension that was vibrating in the air.

The hard masculine line of his mouth curved cynically as he said, 'You do the icy courteous act to perfection. It's been a joy to watch, but, since I happen to know the woman behind the marble façade, you can drop it now.'

'I don't know what you mean.'

'Stop playing games with me, Elin.'

He was pushing her further and further on to the defensive with his methodical attack and, forgetting her resolve to keep her cool, she snapped in retaliation, 'I thought you were the one doing that!'

'Meaning?'

'Meaning that, out of all the boutiques you could have walked into to buy a scarf, why did you pick this one?' she demanded, throwing the words at him.

He smiled sardonically, his tone cutting as he answered, 'Perhaps I had a notion to see Daddy's rich little girl with her latest toy.'

The gloves of politeness were really off now.

'*Toy*?' she echoed, her green eyes ablaze. 'I earn my living from this *toy*, as you call it! And if your implication is that my father bought the boutique for me, you're wrong about that too! I arranged a bank loan so I could acquire the lease.'

'You slipped up, darling,' he mocked, the grooves around his mouth deepening cynically. 'You should have taken Roger for a better divorce settlement. I can only assume you didn't because you thought you'd go running home to your father when your marriage ended, and he'd take care of everything for you.'

'I stand on my own two feet!'

'After a lifetime of being spoilt and pampered?' Garel said with a harsh laugh. 'That's hard to believe!'

'You're rude and arrogant!'

'For pointing out a few home truths?'

She tossed her head back, her green eyes glittering as she retorted, 'Just because you had a hard time when you were growing up, don't you despise me for having a rich father!'

'A father who certainly brought you up with all the right values,' Garel sneered. 'Fidelity being one of them.'

Incredulous that he dared make such a comment, she flashed, 'You damned hypocrite!'

'I have my faults, but hypocrisy isn't listed among them,' he shot back.

At any other time the snap in his voice would have sent a shiver of warning through her, but the pain of the past made her too angry to think of backing down.

'No?' she challenged in a ringing voice. 'Not even when you have the *gall* to stand there and accuse me of infidelity when at the time of our affair you were cheating on your *wife*?'

Garel's black brows came together, disbelief and then fury blazing in his dark eyes. Despite the glass-topped counter that separated them, she took an instinctive step backwards, her heart hammering and her mouth suddenly dry.

Garel stared at her, his face set so hard that it might have been carved out of stone.

'I ought to shake you senseless!' he said, tightly leashed ferocity vibrating his voice.

With angry strides, he crossed the distance to the door, leaving her too stunned by what his fury seemed to convey even to move.

'Garel . . .?' she faltered.

But she was too late. The shop door had already slammed behind him, the bell jangling noisily. She leaned against the counter, her legs trembling. Her mind was a whirl of conflicting thoughts.

It wasn't possible that she had accused him wrongly. Running a distraught hand through her hair, she marshalled the evidence quickly, the photograph she had seen in his wallet, James's comments which had made it sound as though Garel's wife had died only recently. And yet the force of his anger belonged to a man enraged by a false imputation.

She tried to calm her agitated thoughts by telling herself that it didn't matter one way or another. Her affair with Garel belonged to the past, to that part of her life she wanted to forget.

But when she could settle to nothing that evening, she realised that, for some reason, knowing the truth mattered to her very much. She switched on he television, hoping that the highlights of the day's play at Wimbledon might distract her and help her to relax. But before she had time to get interested in the match that was being shown the telephone rang.

She had no reason to expect that Garel would call her, but that didn't stop her heart from jolting. The very way she rose, crossed to the phone and picked up the receiver betrayed that she was apprehensive that it might be him and yet, at the same time, she needed to talk to him.

'Hello?' she began, her voice a shade strained.

'Hello, Elin. It's James here. How's life?'

The tension in her melted and she sank on to the arm of the nearby easy chair.

'I'm fine,' she answered automatically.

'Trade's good, I hope?'

'Yes, at the moment. The lovely weather helps. If it goes on,' she joked lightly, 'I'll have nothing left to put in the summer sale.'

James laughed. 'It sounds to me,' he said, 'as if you're going to keep me busy with your accounts, which is really why I'm phoning. There are one or two points about your VAT returns which I need to clear up before I send them in. I was wondering if we could deal with it over lunch tomorrow.'

'Yes, I can manage that,' she agreed, and was arranging a time with him when it occurred to her that their lunch date would give her the opportunity of establishing whether or not five years ago Garel had been a married man.

Since James was a friend of his, he would be able to settle the question that was tormenting her.

It was just after twelve when he called in at the boutique the next day.

'Where would you like to eat?' he asked as they strolled towards his car that was parked at the top of the sunlit high street.

'Let's make it somewhere near,' she suggested, 'as I'd like to be back at the shop by two. There's a Greek restaurant that's just opened in Northwood which is supposed to be good. Shall we try that?'

James agreed, and they were soon seated at a table in comfortable and elegant surroundings under the watchful eye of a most charming team of solicitous waiters. Over the hors d'oeuvre James sorted out the queries he had mentioned to her on the phone.

The problems were so few that it was obvious he had used them as an excuse for seeing her. James was far too nice for her to want ever to have to rebuff him, but, much as she liked him, she simply wasn't drawn to him romantically.

Hitherto she had been tentative about bringing Garel into the conversation because she didn't want James to question her about her involvement with him. But suddenly she saw that if she did appear interested in Garel that might be the best way of spelling out to James that she valued him as an adviser and friend, but nothing more.

'Guess who came into the boutique yesterday,' she began.

'Some celebrity, a TV personality?' he questioned. 'I know Pinner has more than its quota.'

'No, you're on the wrong lines.'

'Who, then?' he smiled.

'Garel Griffith.'

A quizzical light came into James's eyes as he asked, 'What did he want?'

'To buy a scarf.'

'Ostensibly,' James commented with a frown. 'I think it's more likely myself that he visited the shop to see *you*.' She didn't deny it and he went on, 'Am I right in guessing there was once something between the two of you?'

Fingering the stem of her wine glass, she nodded. Then, raising her eyes to his, she said quietly, 'Which is why I'm interested in knowing more about his wife.'

James's mouth tightened with resignation as he met the unconscious appeal in her gaze.

'You're asking me if he's still in love with her?' he queried. 'It's all so long ago he must be over it by now.'

'*How* long?' she asked, almost inaudibly.

'Let me think,' James mused. 'His wife was killed the same year I passed the last of my accounts exams, so . . . it must be eight years ago this summer.'

Though Elin had speculated on the possibility that she had accused Garel wrongly, the confirmation of it still left her momentarily dazed. She closed her eyes for an instant, her inky lashes fluttering as she fought to master her emotions.

The photograph she had seen that day in his wallet, even after all this time, remained etched vividly in her mind. If only she had questioned him about it, instead of jumping to what then had seemed the obvious conclusion.

In a cramped voice, she asked, 'Who ... who looks after his little boy?'

'Didn't you know?' James sounded puzzled. 'Stephen was killed in the car crash with his mother.'

She stared at him in shock, her eyes darkening. A tide of compassion for Garel swamped her, wiping out completely her own sense of dismay. Her throat felt painfully tight as she whispered, 'Oh, God, to lose both his wife *and* his son! How awful for him!'

'Yes, it was,' James agreed, before adding quietly, 'You must care about him very much.'

Startled, she asked huskily, 'What makes you say that?'

'You're obviously so upset.'

'It's just that I ... I feel so bad about ... about something I said to him yesterday.'

'I'm sure he doesn't hold it against you,' James said. 'He'd realise you didn't know.' Then, when her lack of reply told him she was unconvinced, he suggested, 'Well, then, why don't you call round at his house and explain?'

'I don't have his address,' she shrugged.

'That's easily remedied,' James said. He took out one of his business cards, and commented with rueful humour as he wrote Garel's address on it, 'You're lucky I'm a good loser.'

She reached across the table to put an impulsive hand over his. 'You're a real friend, James,' she said gratefully.

Giving her hand a squeeze, he smiled. 'I hope I always will be,' he said.

# CHAPTER FIVE

ELIN sat on the bed in the evening sunlight blow-drying her hair, her mind full of thoughts. The card James had given her that afternoon with Garel's Moor Park address written on it lay on her dressing-table. It was almost eight o'clock. Should she drive over to see Garel now, or would it be better, perhaps, to wait a day or two?

She ran her fingers through her shiny hair. Feeling only a trace of dampness left from the shower, she switched off the drier. In her lace-trimmed bra and briefs she walked over to the wardrobe to put it away. Then she paused at the open window which overlooked the garden. A faint breeze stirred the net curtains, its caress warm on her bare skin.

She bit her lower lip pensively and then, her mind made up, she turned away from the window. Returning to her wardrobe, she took out a white silk tunic dress with gilt buttons. She would call on Garel this evening while her nerve still held.

When she had changed she sat down at her dressing-table and twisted her hair into a chignon. Freshly washed, it was as slippery as silk, but she wanted to wear it up. She wasn't expecting Garel to make it easy for her to apologise to him, and to stiffen her resolve she needed to know that, outwardly at least, she gave the impression of composure and self-assurance.

His detached house was large and modern and set

well back off the quiet leafy road. She saw that his Jaguar was parked in the circular drive, so knew he must be home.

She drew up on the other side of the road beneath a large horse-chestnut tree and got out, paying little attention to the blue Escort that was parked ahead of her. Butterflies fluttered in her stomach as she walked up the drive and rang the front door bell. Garel didn't answer it immediately and, taking a deep breath to steady her jumping nerves, she was about to press the bell again when the door opened.

Her pulse quickened in response to the tall, arrogantly male figure standing in front of her. Garel was casually dressed, his white Lacoste T-shirt contrasting with the swarthiness of his chiselled features. Jeans hugged his lean hips and emphasised the muscular length of his legs.

At the sight of him, the opening sentence she had rehearsed during the drive went completely out of her head and she began a shade breathlessly, 'Hello, Garel.'

His masculine gaze raked her, a mocking light in his dark eyes as he said with light sarcasm, 'This is unexpected. To what do I owe the honour of a surprise call?'

'I . . . I wanted to talk to you.'

'I'm intrigued,' he said. 'Come on in.'

He stood back for her to enter, and then motioned towards the open door to the lounge. She acknowledged his invitation with a small, tight smile and walked ahead of him into the spacious split-level room.

With patio doors on to a beautifully landscaped garden, it was decorated in beige and rust with

traditional design armchairs that looked well with the
teak furniture. But she had time to form only the
briefest impression of the masculine surroundings
because, to her surprise, she saw that Garel had
company.

Sitting on the sofa was a stunningly attractive
auburn-haired woman in her mid-twenties. She was
wearing a pale blue jacket with a fan-pleated skirt in
a slightly darker shade of the same colour. Knotted
round her throat was the cobalt and amethyst silk scarf.

Elin's eyes glittered as she recognised it. If she'd
had any idea that the red-head on the sofa was the
owner of the Ford Escort she'd seen parked outside
she'd have driven straight on.

Garel, not realising that she'd gone back to her
maiden name, introduced her to the other woman as
Elin Llewellyn. Automatically Elin corrected the
mistake as she and Felicity exchanged greetings.

'Are you on a visit or do you live locally?' Felicity
enquired as she gave Elin a narrowed, measuring-up
glance.

'Locally,' she supplied. 'I live in Pinner.'

Afraid that she might have revealed the dart of
jealousy that had gone through her when she had
walked into the lounge, she was more then ever
determined to appear friendly.

'I thought with names like Hughes and Llewellyn
you must be from somewhere in Wales.'

'I am. I'm from Glasfryn originally, which is near
Dolgellau in North Wales, but I've hardly lived there
since I left college.'

'Elin studied fashion and design. Her father owns a
very successful woollen mill,' Garel amplified.

'And I suppose, as his daughter,' Felicity said, 'you

have a very successful job in it.'

Her slight smile made the delivery of the barbed remark perfect.

'As a matter of fact I don't work in the business,' Elin returned, trying not to glare at her. 'I run a boutique.'

'Oh, you have a little shop,' Felicity said with a rush of patronising charm that was aimed at putting Elin in her place.

'Yes, it's the shop the silk scarf you're wearing came from,' Elin answered sweetly. 'Now I see it with your difficult colouring, I can understand why Garel took so long choosing it for you.'

'It helped having such a patient sales assistant,' Garel said, masculine amusement in his eyes that suggested he appreciated Elin's ability to retaliate in kind.

Yet, although she appeared well able to hold her own with Felicity, she was wishing stormily that she was anywhere but sitting opposite Garel in his lounge. Why ever had he asked her in? Had he wanted to gauge her reaction to meeting the red-head? She felt a swift flaring of antagonism at the thought. There was enough enmity between them from the past for him to enjoy eliciting a spark of jealousy from her.

'Does you husband run the boutique with you?' Felicity asked innocently, as though she'd misunderstood Elin's marital status following their introduction.

'I don't have a husband,' Elin answered.

'She has a cat instead,' Garel commented, a note of easy humour in his voice. 'She's an isolationist.'

'That's rather an exaggeration,' Elin laughed, masking her annoyance at what she suspected was a subtle gibe, 'though I must admit I do find Sam easy to get along with.'

'Meaning that you find people difficult?' Garel enquired, his dark eyes mocking her.

'Only some people,' she told him pointedly.

Despite Felicity's presence, they might have been alone for the undercurrents of confrontation that were beginning to develop between them. Pleased by them, Felicity announced, 'Well, I must leave the two of you to work out the relative merits of cats and people. If it turns out you can make it tomorrow after all, Garel, drop in any time during the evening.'

'Thanks.'

Getting to her feet, she explained breezily to Elin, 'I'm giving a barbecue tomorrow. That's why I want to get my shopping done tonight.'

Garel hadn't exaggerated when he had said that Felicity's eyes were the colour of wild irises, and she felt if she was forced to watch her using them to flirt with him a moment longer she'd explode with temper.

'I'll see you out, Fliss,' Garel said, his pet name for Felicity adding to the note of warmth in his deep voice.

Left alone in the lounge, Elin stood up and paced over to the stone fireplace. Just the thought of him kissing Felicity goodbye made her feel a hot blaze of mutinous anger. She told herself she had no interest whatsoever in Garel's private life, but the self-deception didn't quell the turbulence in her.

When she had pulled up outside his house she'd fully intended explaining to him why, five years ago, she'd made the assumption that he was married, and saying that she was sorry. But now she was changing her mind about confessing to him.

She could imagine his cynical response. He was so

hatefully sarcastic, and had such contempt for her, why should she humble herself to him? Just the brutal arrogance with which he had kissed her on Saturday cancelled out the need for her apology.

There was an angry light in her eyes when he returned to the lounge, having certainly taken his time.

'Well,' he began, 'now that we're alone, satisfy my curiosity. What did you want to talk to me about?'

She pivoted from the fireplace to face him, noting the faintly mocking inclination of his dark head. Hunching her shoulders in an indifferent shrug, she said calmly, determined that he wouldn't know that seeing him with Felicity had evoked any reaction from her, 'It's not important.'

'It is, or you wouldn't have driven round here. And you must have gone to some trouble to find out my address,' he mused, adding quizzically, 'So what prompted such determination to see me?'

'I didn't go to any trouble to get your address,' she lied. 'James mentioned you were living in Moor Park these days when we were having lunch together this afternoon. I happened to be passing, that's all. But if I'd known you were entertaining I wouldn't have called in.'

Garel's gaze narrowed astutely on her face. 'Jealous?' he suggested softly.

She tossed her head back. 'Of Felicity?' she challenged coolly. 'Not at all. Except I wouldn't have thought she was your type.'

He perched on the arm of the sofa, his jeans outlining the strong muscles of his thighs.

'In what way?' he asked blandly.

'Her personality doesn't match her looks.'

A glint of sardonic amusement came into his brown

eyes.

'I had a feeling you hadn't taken to Felicity,' he said, a faint inflexion of satisfaction in his voice. 'Now, what will you have to drink?'

'Nothing, thank you. I'm driving.'

'That doesn't rule out coffee,' he replied, getting up. 'I'll go and plug the percolator in.'

'I don't want coffee.'

'Stop being so unsociable,' he ordered. He paused in the doorway to add with a touch of irony, 'By the way, contrary to the conclusion you've undoubtedly jumped to, Felicity is my PA, not my bed-partner.'

'It's of no consequence to me what your relationship is with Felicity,' she told him coldly.

'No?' Garel queried, quirking a mocking eyebrow at her. 'It was all I could think of to explain why, having been so reasonable when you first arrived, you're suddenly being so unaccountably hostile.'

'I'm not being hostile!'

'In which case, when I bring the coffee in you can tell me what it is you called to see me about.'

He went out, leaving her to walk restlessly over to an armchair. She sat down, fingering the gold chain around her neck. It was illogical, but learning that Felicity was his employee and not his mistress had mollified her slightly. She gave a short sigh as she decided that she was behaving like a fool. She'd resolved to confess to him. The sooner she got it over with the better.

Her nerves tensed as he returned with the coffee. He seemed to dominate the lounge with his virility and the power of his personality. She let her eyes roam over him as he set the percolator down on the coffee-table, her heartbeat quickening.

'How would you like your coffee? Black or white?' he asked.

'Black,' she told him, moistening her lips.

He poured it for her and then handed her the cup. Bracing herself to begin, she reached out for the saucer. As she took it from him her hand accidentally came into contact with his, while at the same moment their eyes met.

A tiny electric shock seemed to go through her, making her fingers jerk. The cup rocked on its saucer, sending some of the nearly boiling coffee over the rim. She gave a stifled cry of pain as the coffee burned her hand.

'Damn! Are you hurt?' Garel asked in concern, shoving the cup on to the coffee-table.

'No, it's nothing,' she said, putting the smarting knuckle of her forefinger to her mouth to try to ease the pain.

'Let me see,' he demanded, taking hold of her wrist. Seeing that her scalded skin was already turning an angry red, he went on, 'You need cold water on that straight away.'

Before she could protest he had her on her feet and, with his palm against her back, he was ushering her from the room. He was so much in charge of the situation that it wasn't until they were in the hall that she said, wincing slightly, 'It's not much. I . . . I can see to it. I'll splash some water on it in the kitchen.'

'No, come upstairs. I've got some burn cream in the medicine cabinet.'

He led the way into his master bedroom and escorted her inside the bathroom that opened off it. Quickly he turned on the cold tap over the washbasin for her. While she stood with the running water gushing over her injured hand he opened the mirrored door to the cabinet.

Unsettled, not only by his nearness but also by her awareness that she was completely alone with him, and that his bedroom lay beyond the door, she edged out of his way. Immediately she felt his glance on her and hoped he would think that her strained expression was caused solely by her scalded hand.

'Is it starting to feel better?' he asked after another minute had passed.

'Yes, it . . . it doesn't burn as it did.'

He turned off the tap and reached for the towel that was hanging in the gold ring next to the basin. Ignoring the way she stretched out her wet hand to take it from him, he began to dry it for her himself.

Not daring to raise her eyes to his face when he was standing so close to her, she watched as he dried her fingers before pressing the soft towel carefully against the tender skin of her knuckles. Against her will the memory of the night five years ago when he had made love to her leapt into prominence in her thoughts. There had been the same knowing gentleness in his hands then. She breathed in sharply as she recalled with disturbing vividness the erotic mastery of his touch.

Immediately he glanced up, his eyes probing hers.

'Is it still painful?'

For a startled instant she thought telepathy had enabled him to read minds. Then, realising he was referring to her hand, not the memories, she blushed and said, 'No . . . I . . .'

'What?' he asked.

'I . . . I was thinking of something else.'

'Something so painful it makes you wince?' he

queried, adding with a touch of sarcasm when she didn't favour him with a reply, 'No point, I suppose, in my asking what it was?'

She shook her head. 'No,' she confirmed tightly. 'May I have the cream?'

'I'll put it on for you.'

'I'd rather put it on myself.'

'Are you so fiercely independent that you hate accepting help, or is it that you don't like me touching you?'

'Of course I don't mind you touch——' She broke off as the sardonic glitter in his eyes made her realise that her remark was open to misinterpretation.

'Then stop shying away,' he ordered.

He began to smooth the cream on to her knuckle, dextrously rubbing it into her skin. Her pulse stirred at the rhythmic caress of his fingers and, before the sensation she both feared and loved could get any stronger, she pulled her hand away.

'That's fine,' she said jerkily. 'It doesn't hurt any more.'

Leaving him to put the tube of cream back in the cabinet, she went quickly to the door. There she paused, hesitating an instant before gathering her determination. Turning, she said in a sudden rush, 'Garel, I . . . I'm sorry for what I said to you in the boutique yesterday. I didn't know about your wife and your little boy being killed in a car crash.'

His jaw tightened as he answered, his tone clipped, 'Evidently.'

Despite his brusque rejection of her apology, she persisted, 'I thought when I met you five years ago that you were single.'

'I *was* single,' he rapped out. 'So what exactly made

you think otherwise?'

'A photograph I saw in your wallet,' she confessed. 'I . . . I found it the morning after . . .'

'After we'd made love?'

His harsh intimate words made her flare, 'Yes, after we'd made love. How do you think I felt when I saw it?'

'Frankly, I've no idea,' he answered, his eyes cold as he strolled towards her. 'The impression you left me with, if you remember, was that you'd had too much to drink, but that one lapse in faithfulness to your fiancé wasn't going to stop you from proceeding with a good marriage.'

Her voice tight, she flashed in self-defence, 'I was hurt! I wanted to hurt you back.'

Garel quirked a sardonic black eyebrow at her.

'Are you telling me that our night together *did* mean something to you after all?'

Conscious of a welling tide of pain inside her that had been repressed for much too long, she cried out, 'Of course it did! I was a virgin when you seduced me!'

The husky catch in her voice made no impression on the hard set of his jaw. 'Poor old Roger,' he said cuttingly, 'cheated of the virgin bride on his wedding night.'

She felt a hot blaze of anger. Hating him at that moment, she hissed, 'Roger *knew*.'

He took hold of her by the wrist, his face dark and cynical. 'Then he was more forgiving than I'd have been,' he rasped. 'In his shoes, I think I'd have killed you.'

'But then you don't know the meaning of the word forgiveness,' she shot back accusingly, furious that when he was so hard and unfeeling she was letting him stir up such a tempest of angry hurt inside her. 'I don't know why I bothered to come here. You've caused me pain enough!'

'What are you talking about?'

'I'm damned if I'm going to tell you,' she snapped. 'You're arrogant, hard and self-righteous, and I don't care any more what you think about me, or the way I behaved.'

She whirled away, closer suddenly to tears than she wanted him to see. He recaptured her almost immediately. Taking hold of her chin with determined fingers, he forced her to meet his smouldering gaze.

A quiver of trepidation ran along her spine. Far from being indifferent to what she was saying, she saw from the nerve that jumped in his jaw that he was furious.

'What am I supposed to think?' he demanded. 'You knew I was attracted to you. You found me attractive, too, admit it. Come on, I want you to admit it.'

His hands moved to grip her shoulders when she didn't answer him promptly, and he gave her a shake so that she cried, 'Yes, I found you attractive!'

'But you still went ahead quite calmly and married your fiancé,' he said in a voice that bit with scorn.

'No, I didn't ,' she burst out angrily. 'Not in the way you're implying.'

'You mean you actually did some heart-searching?' he jeered.

'I did more than some heart-searching,' she said on a rising note. 'I broke off my engagement because I slept with you!'

Garel's hawkish eyes narrowed on her, the belief that flickered in their depths snuffed out the next instant by scepticism.

'Since you married your fiancé the following Easter, that's a little hard to believe,' he said harshly. 'I saw the announcement in *The Times*, which was why I sent you what seemed to be an appropriate wedding present.'

'Think what you like,' she flashed back, tired of trying to justify herself, 'including, if you want, that I'm easy to see through.'

'Oh, no,' he said with flinty determination. 'You don't get this far without telling me what happened.'

'Let go of me!' she demanded. Two of the pins fell out of her hair as she tried to wrench herself free from him, the weight of her chignon loosening the rest. It cascaded about her shoulders as she went on, 'I've tried to talk to you, but you're not prepared to listen, and I no longer want to explain.'

'You're wrong, Elin,' he snapped, clamping hold of both her wrists. 'I want to listen very much.'

Imprisoned too ruthlessly for there to be any point in continuing to struggle, she hissed angrily, 'No, you don't. You're not prepared to listen at all.'

'Try me.'

'Why should I, when you think I'm a cold-hearted bitch?'

'Five years ago you seemed determined to give me that impression,' he reminded her gratingly.

Her gaze faltered and, as her defiance crumbled, the cruelty of his grip eased.

'I've already told you why that was,' she mumbled.

'Then tell me the rest of it.'

Her eyes returned to him as she declared, 'Not here in your bedroom.'

'Does being with me in a bedroom disturb you?' he asked with dry mockery.

She coloured a little. 'No,' she denied, 'but it's hardly the best place to talk.'

'And you'd feel safer downstairs,' he surmised, adding, 'In which case we'll finish this conversation in the lounge.'

He stood back for her to precede him. She didn't want to have to tell him any more. Her strained nerves were already raw, but to put up resistance at this point was impossible. A covert glance at the determined line of his jaw as he entered the lounge told her that.

'You look very pale,' he said, his tone a shade clipped. 'Are you sure you won't change your mind about a drink?'

She drew a deep breath. 'I'll have a Campari and lemonade, if you've got it.'

He fixed her drink and then poured himself a whisky. As he handed her glass to her he prompted, 'You said you broke off your engagement to Roger.'

On the defensive with him, she thought he was doubting her word and retorted, 'I did!'

'Then how come you went ahead and married him?' Garel asked as he sat down in a nearby armchair. There was something taut in his face, but with her eyes on the drink in her hands she didn't see it. 'Did you discover you were in love with him after all?'

'Yes . . . no . . .' she faltered, setting her drink down untouched and pushing her hand through her hair. 'I was fond of him and . . . and I thought he needed me. When he was ill with viral pneumonia and I sat by his bedside I . . . I realised I still cared about him.'

Garel kept his hard, expressionless gaze on her as he lifted his whisky glass to his mouth. The strong muscles of his throat flexed as he took a swallow.

'When was this?' he asked.

'The November after I'd broken off my engagement to him,' she said. She got to her feet and paced over to the glass doors that overlooked the garden. With her back to him, she hugged her arms. Her voice was cramped as she went on, 'It was awful. I got to the hospital and he was so ill, so much worse than I'd ever expected.'

'You mean you thought he wasn't going to pull through?' Garel questioned.

She nodded. 'The doctors weren't at all hopeful. It seems that Roger had been overworking and was completely run down.'

'And you felt responsible,' he guessed drily.

'I not only felt responsible, but his mother told me I was in so many words. She said that . . .' Elin's voice wavered and she paused to steady it. 'She said that if Roger died it would be because I'd destroyed him.'

She heard Garel set his glass down. 'Roger's mother was distraught,' he said impatiently as he got to his feet. 'Surely your father told you that?'

'No, he didn't,' she said, pivoting to face him. 'Dad had no idea why I'd broken off the engagement, and he'd always liked Roger. He didn't say it, but deep down I knew he blamed me too.'

'So, with the weight of opinion from all sides against you, when Roger asked you to reconsider you said yes.'

'It wasn't like that. I didn't say yes because I was pressurised by his family, or by my father. I said yes because I wanted to share my life with Roger. When he was out of danger I cried, I was so relieved and happy.'

'So it was while he was still in hospital that he asked you to marry him.'

Her throat felt tight and she nodded mutely before saying, 'I'd told him I'd had an affair with someone when I'd broken off our engagement. At the time he'd been furious, but when he proposed to me again he said he'd forgiven me, that he'd never hold it against me or reproach me with it after we were married.'

'Did he?'

'Did he what?' she asked, stalling for time as she suddenly saw where the conversation was leading.

'Subsequently reproach you. Was that what was at the root of your divorce?'

In fact, Roger had kept his word, but, unwilling to tell Garel or anyone else, apart from her father, who knew the whole story, why she had broken up with her husband, she turned away and said, 'It's all water under the bridge now.'

Garel's jaw tightened at her reply. There was a short silence and then he said, sarcasm vibrating his voice, 'I don't suppose it ever occurred to you that the intelligent thing to have done when you saw the photograph of Carol was to ask me about it.'

Both his tone and the anger she saw in the chiselled lines of his swarthy, dominant face took her by surprise. An instant ago they'd been talking like two reasonable people. Now they were glaring at each other again, her own temper quickly catching fire from his.

'There's just no mollifying you, is there?' she flashed. 'If you'd been open with me I wouldn't have jumped to the conclusion that I did. Before you start judging me, why don't you consider for a moment how things looked from my angle? I'd no idea you'd been married but that your wife was dead. When I saw the photograph I thought you'd been amusing yourself with me while she was away. Plenty of married men cheat on their wives. I thought——'

'And you thought I was one of them,' he snapped.

'I made a mistake,' she said, throwing out her hands in entreaty. 'I've told you, I was hurt and I acted stupidly. I was young and I had too much pride to break down in front of you in tears and bitter accusations. I didn't know how to handle the situation.'

'What a masterly understatement!'

'I'd no idea what our night together meant to you.' She continued to defend herself. 'I've still no idea.'

'As you say, it's a lot of water under the bridge,' he said in the same sarcastic tone. 'We'll never know how our relationship might have developed had you not gone rifling through my wallet.'

'I didn't go rifling through your wallet,' she denied, stung by his accusation. 'It fell out of your inside pocket when I picked your jacket up off the floor!'

Garel kept his hard gaze on her. Then, letting it swing away, he drew a deep breath as though the anger was slowly draining out of him.

Her tense shoulders relaxed as she realised that their stormy confrontation had at last raged itself out. Yet the atmosphere was still highly charged, and, needing to get away from it before her poise splintered, she murmured, 'Well, I've apologised, which is what I came here to do, and now it's time I was going.'

Garel's dark brows came together, a knowing light in his brown eyes as they met hers. 'Why don't you drop your guard, Elin?' he mocked.

'What do you mean?' she asked suspiciously.

He advanced towards her, his pace unhurried, the snug fit of his jeans emphasising his lithe, pantherish walk.

'I don't doubt the apology was part of it,' he said, 'but don't tell me you called round solely to clear yourself of accusing me falsely over something that happened five years ago.'

Tall, solid and compellingly attractive, he halted in front of her. His T-shirt was open at the neck, and her pulse seemed to flicker as she noted the dark hairs that curled on his chest. Forcing herself to hold her ground, she challenged, not realising that the very lift of her chin was a dare to his virility, 'What other reason could I have had?'

A brief sardonic smile deepened the grooves around his hard, sensual mouth.

'How about that you wanted to rake over the embers of our relationship to see if there were any sparks left which might be rekindled?' he suggested.

She would have given him an instant fiery denial had not her gaze at that moment clashed with his. The smouldering light in the depths of his eyes made her suddenly breathless. She shied away in panic as he took a step towards her, but he was too quick for her, and, cornered before she could escape, she snapped, 'How typical of your conceit! There aren't any sparks left between us.'

He put a hand against the wall level with her head, leaning towards her, imprisoning her with his hard man's body.

'Aren't there?' he taunted softly.

'Get away from me,' she demanded, infuriated by his sexual advance.

He shook his head, the set of his jaw ruthless and determined for all his relaxed manner. 'Not this time,' he said studying her turbulent green eyes and the angry flush along her classical cheekbones. 'And you know why? Because I'm not convinced you really mean it. In fact, I'm beginning to wonder just why it is you keep giving me come-on signals only to cancel them out the next minute.'

'That's a lie!' she flashed.

He grazed a caressing finger down her cheek, making her recoil with a sharp catch of breath.

'Is it?' he said speculatively. 'I don't think so. I'd say that underneath that haughty façade and those sudden flashes of temper there's a scared little cat. Why is that, Elin? Why should the prospect of just one kiss excite and frighten you so much?'

She saw what he was driving at and her heart began to race as she tried to deny inwardly what he was saying. She had vowed never to make herself vulnerable by falling in love again. As much to reassure herself as to convince him, she leaned back against the wall and gazed up at him, her green eyes limpid and faintly mocking.

'I'm a worldly-wise twenty-five, Garel. Do you really think I'm frightened of a kiss?' she asked lazily.

'Then prove it,' he commanded, a husky note in his charismatic voice. 'Kiss me.'

He didn't move, yet the masculinity that emanated from him was so powerful that his very stillness seemed a threat. The bracing fragrance of his aftershave stirred her senses. Her pulse quickened, drumming loudly in her ears as her eyes travelled to his firm, sensual mouth that was as blatantly male as the rest of him.

It was pure bravado that prompted her to match her actions to her words. Giving him a faint bewitching smile, she fitted her hand to the chiselled line of his jaw. Moving forward on to her toes, she kissed first

one and then the other corner of his mouth, attempting
only to meet his dare, not to satisfy.

When she drew back it was to see a dark fire
glowing in his eyes.

'Now let's try it with a little passion,' he muttered.

Her lips parted to protest, but before she could utter
a sound he had bent his head, engulfing her in his
embrace. She clutched at his shoulders as he claimed
her mouth in a hungry, searching kiss, evoking from
her a response so acute that she thought she was
falling.

Drowning in a wave of feeling, she threaded her
fingers into the raven thickness of his hair. He
deepened the kiss and at the same time pulled her into
a still more intimate fit against him. She was able to
feel the size and strength of his powerful aroused body
with every inch of her; a shiver of sexual hunger went
through her and, shocked, she broke the kiss.

'That's enough!' she said shakily.

'Not for me, it isn't.'

'You've had your kiss. Now let me go,' she flared,
frightened by the force field of sexual magnetism that
threatened to ensnare her. 'I don't intend letting what
happened between us five years ago repeat itself!'

'Nor do I.' His voice was husky and compelling.

Their gaze locked for a quivering moment before he
bent his head again.

# CHAPTER SIX

SENSUAL longing flared under the expert persuasion of Garel's mouth, the wildfire that raced along Elin's veins melting what little resistance remained. She moaned softly as he slid a caressing hand up between her shoulder-blades, pressing her breasts to the hard strength of his chest.

A whirlpool of desire had her spinning. The feel of his mouth on hers, and his arms that held her so possessively, were unleashing emotions she was helpless to control. It was as if all the power of her femininity, that she had kept suppressed for so long, now surged into life, making her response to him as ardent as it was unbidden. His kiss seemed to go on forever, intimate, demanding, insatiable, and long before it was over she was curved pliantly against him, her fingers threading into his dark hair as she kissed him back.

When he raised his head her inky lashes slowly fluttered upwards to see him looking down at her, his expression intent as he noted with masculine satisfaction the soft fullness of her lips and the hot glow in the depths of her eyes. The icy façade had cracked wide open, revealing the elemental and vulnerable woman within.

'That was nice,' he whispered, his breathing as altered as her own. 'We must try it again soon.'

The smile he gave her was as devastatingly sensual as his thumb that gently caressed her cheek. It was his words which broke the spell.

She stared up at him in mounting consternation, aware that her face was flushed and that her hands were still linked behind his neck. What had she given away when she had been in his arms? No man had ever been able to excite her the way he did, making her drown in feelings that swept the world away.

When he had kissed her she had been able to think of nothing save the flames of pleasure that had flickered hungrily along her nerves. She had wanted him. She still wanted him, and the knowledge was far more than she could cope with.

In a shaken whisper, she said, 'I don't intend either seeing you or kissing you again.'

His mouth tightened. 'Stop being a fool, Elin,' he commanded. 'The chemistry between us is as strong as it was five years ago, and you know it.'

She felt her heartbeat quicken. Total self-sufficiency was the cornerstone of the life she had built for herself since her divorce. She refused to surrender it to any man by getting involved in a relationship. Yet in two years her emotions had never been under attack as suddenly as they were now.

Afraid of what Garel was saying, she flashed defensively, 'There's no such thing as chemistry and, even if there were, it's not what I'm looking for. I know what you think, but you're wrong. I didn't come here with the aim of rekindling our relationship.'

'You're lying,' he shot back, 'not just to me, but to yourself.'

'You've had your kiss, which was what you wanted,' she said stormily. 'Now let me go.'

She felt his fingers tighten painfully on her shoulders, and knew by some strange instinct that the action was involuntary.

'You know damn well what I want,' he growled, his smouldering gaze compelling hers. 'And you also know damn well that neither of us is satisfied.'

Hot colour came into her face. He was too direct, too devastatingly candid. He still held her trapped against the wall, his body in intimate proximity with hers, and she had to fight the impulse to hit out at him in an effort to free herself. There was too much sexual static in the air for her to want to struggle with him. Intuition warned her that if she did she might unleash something in both of them that had been lurking not far beneath he surface ever since they had met at James's party.

With her heart pounding, she lifted her chin a fraction, keeping her voice chill as she said, 'Speak for yourself. And now, unless you intend forcing yourself on me, I'd be grateful if you'd let me go.'

Something glittered in the depths of his eyes for an instant. But to her relief he drew back, a brief sardonic smile touching his mouth.

'Like all wild things, you're easily scared, aren't you?' he said softly. 'And you don't like feeling cornered.'

She hated him for being perceptive enough to have fathomed the timidity that lay behind her cool words. In one evening he had compelled her to reveal far too much about herself. With empty defiance, she said, 'You don't know anything about me.'

'Then let's change that,' he said. 'Have dinner with me tomorrow night.'

His invitation took her by surprise. She gazed back at him, noting the ebony blackness of his hair, the aggressive thrust of his jaw, the attractive grooves on either side of his resolute mouth. Every feature was utterly male, while the same raggedness and virility was stamped in every line of his lean, powerful body

Her shattering awareness of him alarmed her, as did the determination and ruthlessness she sensed in him. Her every instinct was to run before, against her will, she became involved with him.

'I . . . I already have plans,' she lied.

'Cancel them,' he said implacably.

'Don't you know a refusal when you hear one?'

'When I hear one,' he agreed.

That he should have divined her slight hesitation threw her into a panic. Her voice rising, she retorted, 'I don't want to have dinner with you. Despite your arrogant assumptions, I don't want to see you again. I'm happy with my life the way it is. I want to be left alone. Now can't you understand that?'

She saw his mouth thin into a hard, angry line. For a brief moment he seemed to have to fight his frustration with her, and then he relaxed. His sudden change of attitude perplexed her, as did the attractive smile he gave her.

'There's a lot I don't understand about you, Elin,' he said softly. 'But I'm glad you called round. At least we've solved part of the mystery.' He bent to place a gentle kiss on her cheek as he added, 'Drive home safely.'

She stared at him in bemusement before seizing her chance and fleeing to the front door. She ran to her car, not needing to glance over her shoulder as she ducked inside to know that he was leaning in the doorway, watching her with measured thoughtfulness.

Trembling slightly, she pulled away with a roar of acceleration. She was certain he was playing some kind of game with her. Garel wasn't the sort of man to give up on anything, whether it was a business deal he had set out to capture, or a woman. She didn't trust the way he had suddenly backed off. What next move was he planning?

She shouldn't have called to see him. He'd misconstrued her motives, and now she'd opened a floodgate of trouble for herself. But the fact was, she *had* called to see him.

She took a deep breath as she tried to calm her agitated thoughts. He had asked her to have dinner with him and she had refused. If he asked her again her answer would still be the same. In the face of complete indifference, not even a man as determined as Garel would persist. He would have to leave her in peace.

Aware that her lips still recalled the magic of his mouth on hers, she brushed her fingers against them to erase the sensation. As she did so the question formed in her mind before she was able to suppress it. Was it realistic to think that she would remain indifferent to the man who had stirred her so deeply five years ago, who stirred her with the same intensity now? He only had to touch her to make her feel weak.

She tightened her grip on the steering-wheel. She had to fight against what she felt for him. No man was going to storm the citadel of her emotions, and especially not a man with a temper that matched her own.

She slept badly, not just that night, but the following night as well. She jerked suddenly into consciousness in her single bed, hearing the echo of her frightened cry. Her eyes were full of fear and her breathing ragged as she sat up. Then, as she realised it was only a nightmare, that Roger wasn't raging at her, she sank back against the pillows with relief.

The sun was up behind the drawn curtains and she let her gaze wander over the familiar items of her bedroom, her pulse beginning to slow to its normal pace. It was some while since she had been troubled by that particular nightmare. She supposed that arguing with Garel had somehow triggered off memories of the fights she had had with her ex-husband after he had been drinking.

Feeling shaken, she pushed back the covers and slid out of bed. Her pale green silk wrap was draped over a nearby chair, and she pulled it on. The dawn had only just come, but she knew she would find it hard to drift back to sleep again, and she didn't want to lie awake dwelling on her disastrous marriage.

She went downstairs and made herself a pot of tea while her cat rubbed affectionately round her ankles. She fed him, let him out, and then wandered into the lounge where she kicked off her satin mules. Curling up on the sofa, she sipped her hot tea slowly.

It was very early and the garden was full of sunlight and sharp, slanting shadows. Sam went leaping across the lawn, chasing two cabbage-white butterflies which danced above his head just out of reach. She smiled at his antics and then sighed, realising how still and oppressively quiet the house was. She suddenly felt very alone, and then was annoyed with herself because she was used to being alone.

Unbidden, Garel came into her thoughts. He disturbed her. She had no intention of getting involved in either a casual or a permanent relationship, and yet she couldn't stop herself speculating on exactly what it was he wanted from her.

She remembered the siren in the provocative white dress he had spent so much time with at James's party. Then there was Felicity. He obviously wasn't short of women in his life, women who would leap at the chance of an affair with him. Was that what made her different? Did he find her a challenge?

She leaned her head back against the sofa. The sun through the french windows was warm on her skin. It was eight years since Garel's wife had died. There was little doubt that in that time he could have married again ten times over if he'd had a mind to. It made her believe that he must still be in love with his wife, that his only interest in her was sexual. She closed her eyes, her thoughts beginning to eddy as she tried to put him out of her mind.

It was the persistent sound of the doorbell ringing that woke her. Slightly dazed, she opened her eyes. The parallelogram of sunlight had advanced far across the room. She glanced quickly at the carriage clock on the mantelpiece, aghast to see that it was almost a quarter to eleven. By dozing off on the sofa she had slept most of the morning away.

Sweeping her tousled hair away from her face, she stood up. She could see only one of her mules. She must have kicked the other under the valance of the sofa. The bell rang again and, without stopping to hunt for her lost mule, she went barefoot into the hall to answer it.

Her heart seemed to lurch as she saw Garel, the sunlight gleaming on the blackness of his hair. He stood framed in the opening, tall and vitally male, in a cream and black cotton-knit sweater and dark trousers. Instinctively her hand went to her throat to draw the lapels of her wrap more tightly together.

His alert brown eyes registered a glitter of masculine amusement at her reaction. He allowed his gaze to linger for an instant on her silky tousled hair before letting it travel down her slender neck to the hollow of her throat. It didn't stop there, but swept over the diaphanous material of her wrap before returning to her face again.

'Good morning,' he began lazily. 'You know, I'd almost forgotten how bewitching you look when you're in disarray.'

Annoyed to find that she was blushing and challenged, as always, by the raw male sensuality of his presence, she flared, 'If you've come here to make blatant sexual remarks——'

'I haven't,' he interrupted, cutting her short. 'I came here to make sure you were OK.'

Her hand remained at her throat, gripping the wrap's lapels, but her voice was a little less hostile.

'I'm fine,' she said. 'Why shouldn't I be?'

'You were obviously upset on Friday?'

'Whose fault was that?'

'Let's not get on contentious ground immediately,' he said with a touch of humour. 'How's your hand?'

'It's healing up well, thank you. It . . . it was nice of you to call.'

She was genuinely touched by his concern. Had she not been so scantily dressed she would have asked him in, but barefoot and clad only in the flimsy silk of her nightgown and matching wrap she felt too conscious of her femininity. It put her at a disadvantage with him.

A faint smile touched the corners of his firm mouth.

'Are you really so wary of me,' he mocked, 'that you daren't ask me in?'

'I can't. I'm not dressed,' she said.

'That doesn't worry me,' he drawled.

'It may not, but it worries *me*,' she said in a clipped voice. 'I'm grateful to you for calling round, but——'

'Unless you want your neighbours to have something to gossip about, I suggest you change your mind and ask me in,' he interrupted her. 'We have things to talk about.'

The forcefulness of his character was such that she knew he meant it. Despising herself for backing down when she'd made the resolution not to get involved with him, she said, 'You don't give up, do you?'

'Not when I want something.'

Her eyes a shade stormy, she took a step back, turning to walk into the lounge, while he followed.

'You said you wanted to talk to me,' she began. 'What about?'

'You know what about,' he returned quietly.

Suddenly unable to meet his hawkish dark eyes, she glanced away. She was very drawn to him, but her emotional independence was too valuable to her for her to want to give it up. Refusing to confront the issue, she said, 'If I did, I wouldn't ask.'

At that he strode across the room, a frown of irritation between his brows as he tilted her chin up, forcing her to meet his gaze. Her breathing quickened as their eyes locked and some of the harshness left his expression as he noted it.

'Half the time you spend running away from me and the other half you spend bluffing,' he said musingly. 'Now why?'

'If you think I'm a coward and a liar, what are you doing here?' she asked with a flash of spirit.

He quirked a sardonic black brow at her.

'Perhaps because you're an enigma and as such you

intrigue me,' he answered. 'Now, are you going to offer me coffee?'

'Garel, please,' she pleaded, 'I told you on Friday, this is no use.'

'You don't mean that,' he answered, his palms coming to rest lightly on her shoulders.

Through the thin fabric of her wrap his touch warmed her skin. The pleasurable sensation made her quick to flare, 'Don't tell me what I mean. Now take you hands off me. I'm going to get dressed.'

'Don't bother on my account,' he said, a glitter of passion in the depths of his eyes. 'I like looking at you in gossamer silk and lace. It brings back memories.'

The sensual note in his voice quickened her pulse.

'You may want to remember,' she snapped, 'but I don't.'

'Why not?' he demanded. 'Do the memories of what we were like together disturb you so much?'

As he spoke his fingers tightened on her shoulders. She felt the tension between them, the dangerous sexual awareness that filled the air with electricity. He had only to bend his head, she realised, and his lips would claim hers.

'Why are you doing this to me?' she asked on a note of desperation. 'Why can't you just go away and leave me alone?'

'The answer's simple,' he said, his eyes holding hers. 'I care about you.'

Her breath caught in her throat. She was unable to answer, and the racking moment dragged on. Then, just as the air seemed about to snap with static, the telephone started ringing.

Released suddenly from the tension that held her in thrall, she whirled away from him to answer it. Her hand shook slightly as she picked up the receiver to hear her father's rich Welsh voice.

'Hello, Elin. Is everything all right?'

'Yes, fine.'

'I thought you sounded a bit strained when you answered the phone.'

She watched almost warily as Garel prowled over to the french windows and stood staring out at the garden, his hands thrust into the pockets of his trousers. His back was to her and her gaze took in his dark head, the breadth of his shoulders, his lean hips and long legs.

His stance was aggressive, masculinity stamped into every line of him. Forcing herself to relax, she answered her father, 'I've only just woken up. I had a long day in the boutique yesterday.'

'Business must be brisk.'

'It is,' she agreed, a smile in her voice, 'but not so brisk that I can't leave things in Miriam's hands next weekend. I thought I'd get away from here on Friday about four so I should be home in time for a late dinner.'

'I was looking forward to seeing you,' her father said, 'but . . . there's a snag that's cropped up.'

'What's that?' she asked. 'Have you got to be away on business next weekend?'

'No, it's not that,' he said slowly.

'What, then?' she asked with a puzzled laugh. 'Why are you being so mysterious, Dad?'

There was a pause, and then her father said, 'Before you come home next weekend there's something you need to know. Roger's in Glasfryn.'

Her hand tightened on the receiver. Cold with dismay, she echoed, the colour draining from her face,

'In Glasfryn?'

Hearing the catch in her voice, Garel's gaze swung towards her.

'Yes, he arrived last night,' her father said. 'I'm sorry, love. I knew the news would upset you.'

She sat down on the arm of a nearby chair, the silken cascade of hair that fell forward past her cheeks shielding her from Garel's scrutiny. As though he was aware that she was constrained by his presence, he opened the french windows and strolled out on to the patio. Her cat was lying in the sun and he stooped to stroke him.

Able now to give her full attention to the phone call, Elin asked huskily, clutching at straws, 'Are you certain? I mean, you've seen him?'

'Yes, I've seen him. He had the bare-faced audacity to call on me,' her father said, a note of curbed anger in his voice. 'He demanded your address. It seems he's intent on seeing you again.'

'You didn't tell him where I'm living, did you?'

'Of course not,' her father reassured her quickly. 'He got nothing out of me, not a thing. It was all I could do not to give him the hiding he deserved.'

Pushing a harassed hand through her hair, she said, 'I never thought he'd come looking for me. Is . . . is he home for good?'

'No, I asked him about that. He's here for a long holiday. He's still working at the university in Vancouver, but he won't be returning to Canada until September.'

She bit her lip. That meant she had over a month to avoid him. Partly in an attempt to convince herself, and partly because she didn't want her father to worry about her, she said, 'It was probably only a whim on his part to try to see me while he's here. After all, why should he want to contact me? We've been divorced for two years. He must know it's over between us.'

'Well, anyway, I warned him to stay away from you,' her father said grimly. 'If not, he'll have me to answer to.'

His words made her feel safer. Determined to keep Roger's visit to Glasfryn in proportion, she turned the conversation to other topics. She chatted to her father for some time, and then, telling him not to expect her next weekend, she rang off.

She was standing with her hands crossed to hug her arms when Garel paused on the threshold of the french windows. Her back was to him and he studied her for a moment before advancing into the room. Lost in thought, she started as a pair of strong, knowing hands descended on her shoulder, massaging the tension from her neck.

'What is it, Elin?' he asked gently. 'What's wrong?'

She felt the hard strength of his tall, powerful frame behind her. Unsettled by what her father had told her, for an instant she wanted nothing more than to turn into his arms, to feel herself dwarfed by the width of his shoulders as she pressed her cheek against his chest. It was only by a sheer effort of will that she didn't give in to the impulse.

Five years ago she had known Garel to be a strong and dominant personality. Now she was learning about the caring side to his nature. Her vulnerability seemed to draw out in him the need to protect.

Her throat tight, she drew away from him and said, 'Nothing . . . Nothing's wrong.'

He considered her with slightly narrowed eyes, but instead of pressing her for a more candid answer he said, 'Have lunch with me. You look as if you need to unwind and I know just the right place on the river.'

Refusing to allow a moment's weakness to destroy the defences she had built up against him, she answered, 'I'm afraid I can't. I have some bookwork to catch up on.'

'All work and no play——'

'Make for a successful business,' she cut across him.

'But a dull woman,' he fired back.

Strangely, his words cut a little, though she was careful not to let him see it. With a slight lift of her chin, she replied, 'Then I won't inflict my company on you.'

An amused smile deepened the grooves in his tanned cheeks.

'The only time I find you remotely tedious is when you're being obstinate,' he said. He glanced at his watch and went on lazily, 'I'll give you half an hour to get changed. After that I'm coming upstairs to help you.'

She steeled herself to stand firm both against his virility and his forcefulness.

'Don't think you can bully me,' she said. 'I've already told you——'

'For God's sake,' he exploded, his patience finally exhausted. 'Must you fight me every inch of the way?'

'Yes!'

At her defiant rejoinder he caught hold of her by the forearms and pulled her none too gently to his chest. Her heart seemed to skip a beat in response to his nearness.

'You've got two choices, *cariad*,' he said quietly. 'Either you go upstairs and get dressed so that I can

take you out to lunch, or I slip this robe off your
creamy white shoulders and start to make love to you.'

Her lips parted slightly, a flush of heat enveloping
her just at the thought of him carrying out his threat.
She saw his gaze travel to the pulse that beat at the
base of her throat and capitulated quickly, 'I'll . . . I'll
go and get changed.'

'I thought you might,' he mocked softly.

Releasing her, he lifted her hand to his lips to kiss
her palm. The touch of his mouth on her skin sent a
shiver through her. Breathing rapidly, she pulled away
from him. With her wrap held tightly to her, she sped
to the door, hoping that her exit didn't look quite like
the wild flight it was.

In the sanctuary of her bedroom she paced about for
a moment or two before even thinking of getting ready.
It wasn't a lack of courage this time which had made
her give in to him. She had consented to go out to lunch
because deep down she knew she wanted to be with
him.

With a sigh she sat down at her dressing-table,
meeting the steady green eyes that gazed back at her
from the mirror. The truth was that Garel represented
some kind of destiny for her and, sooner or later,
whatever the risk of getting hurt, she was going to have
to accept that fact.

When she came downstairs some while later she
was wearing a sleeveless batik-print dress in beige and
coral which showed off her tanned arms and legs to
advantage. It was nipped in at the waist with a narrow
beige belt that toned well with her Italian leather
sandals. In its very skimpy casualness, the dress was
stylish and eye-catching.

Garel was waiting for her, idly flicking through the

*Radio Times* that lay on the coffee-table. He glanced up as she entered, his eyes assessing her appreciatively from head to foot.

'Ready with five minutes to spare,' he commented, quirking a dark brow at her. 'You must have really believed me when I told you if you took longer than half an hour I'd come up to help you.'

His voice was teasing, coaxing a reluctant smile out of her.

'I never take unnecessary chances,' she joked.

'So I've noticed,' he remarked with dry humour, getting to his feet to escort her to his car.

The restaurant he drove them to was just outside Marlow and fronted directly on to the river. A table out of doors, the bright sunlight and the gentle chug of the passing cruisers combined to create a relaxed mood. In the distance the rolling countryside stretched away, the fields of barley a rich deep gold. From around them came the murmur of talk and laughter from other tables.

All in all it was a perfect lunch with excellent food, chilled wine and conversation that stayed on the general topics of travel, music and shared interests. It surprised her how much they had in common. Without realising it she had relaxed in his company, laughing more than she had in a long while.

They were lingering over coffee, and she was watching some ducks that had come waddling up the bank to be fed on fragments of a roll by a couple who were sitting at a nearby table, when Garel said, 'Now let's talk about us.'

'What about us?' she asked, her gaze coming quickly back to him.

'I want to know why you're so reluctant to get

involved with me,' he said bluntly. 'Is it because of James?'

'I've told you, James is only a friend.'

'Not your lover as well?' he queried, an edge of hardness in his voice.

She slapped her napkin down on the white cloth. 'You have no right——' she began in an angry undertone.

His hand closed firmly on her wrist. It was clear that he intended to tolerate no evasion from her even before he said, 'I have every right. Now stop being so defensive.'

'I . . . I'm sorry,' she murmured.

'OK, let's start again. Am I right in thinking there's been no one in your life since your divorce?'

'That's the way I like things. But before you go on quizzing me there are a couple of questions I'd like to ask you in return.'

'Go ahead.'

'Why do you care whether I'm seeing anyone or not?' she asked. 'It's five years since . . . since our night together, and you don't strike me as a man who's ever short of women's company.'

'I thought I'd answered that,' he replied. 'You intrigue me.'

'As I'm sure plenty of other women have intrigued you over the years,' she commented.

'Some women interest me more than others,' he answered evenly. 'But if you're asking me if there's been anyone special since my wife died, the answer is no, there hasn't.'

He paused, his eyes holding hers, his swarthy, attractive face set in the resolute lines she knew so well as he continued, 'I'm thirty-five. I have my own company, a house worth six hundred thousand pounds and a weekend cottage in Wales. Both in the business world and in financial terms I've been highly successful.' It was said with neither arrogance, nor conceit, simply as a statement of fact. 'But it's not enough,' he went on. 'There's a gap in my life, a gap I now want to fill.'

Her pulse quickened. His train of thought was as clear to her as if he'd said the words out loud.

'I can't help you fill that gap, Garel,' she said.

'Can't?'

'Won't.' The temptation of what he was offering her was too great. She had to reject it quickly. It would be heartbreak all the way to love and marry a man knowing she would never be first in his life. He'd made it plain enough that he would never feel for any woman what he'd felt for Carol. She hurried on, 'If it's a wife and a family you want, you'll have to look elsewhere.'

'Isn't a home and a family what *you* wanted not so very long ago?'

'Five years ago. That's a long time. I've changed since then. I like the life I've built for myself. I'm perfectly content.'

'Are you?' he said, his intonation telling her that he knew far too much about her emotions.

She didn't want him to confuse her like this. She clenched her hands, ignoring the ache beneath her ribs as she answered emphatically. 'Yes. I've tried marriage once and it didn't work. I'm not such a fool that life's taught me nothing, and one of the things I've learned is that a woman is best off on her own.'

'Some of the things life teaches us have to be unlearned,' he fired back.

'What do you mean?'

'Let's take your cat as an example. He's had to unlearn being afraid of people. It wouldn't make much sense for him still to be cowering in an alley when you're prepared to offer him a home.'

'That's a crazy illustration and, in any case, I'm not a stray looking for a warm fireside. Furthermore, regaining trust takes time.'

She realised she had told him a lot with that final sentence—more than she had meant to. There was a short silence while he studied her. Then he asserted quietly, 'I can be patient when the need arises.'

She was silent for much of the drive back. The sun-roof was open, and the noise of the slipstream as they sped along the motorway would have made conversation difficult even had she not been waging a silent war with her emotions.

Her gaze flickered to his profile as she tried to guess his mood. She had categorically refused his offer of marriage. Yet he still gave the impression of flinty determination coupled with total relaxation.

She couldn't fathom him. Much less could she understand herself. If she was so convinced she had made the right decision, why was she feeling so totally bereft and close to tears?

They arrived back at her house where he saw her to the door, claiming her mouth in a brief parting kiss.

'I'll be in touch soon,' he said.

He went to go back down the drive and, fully intent on telling him he was wasting his time, that there was no future in their relationship, she called his name. He turned and enquired, 'Yes?'

To her consternation she somehow couldn't force the words to come. She pleaded huskily, her inner turmoil reflected in her tear-bright eyes, 'Garel, please don't call me. I . . .'

He tilted her chin up, silencing her faltering entreaty as he brushed her lips with his own.

'I said, I'll be in touch,' he repeated softly.

With that he strode off down the drive while she let herself into her house, banging the door shut behind him. Damn him for his determination and virility! She leaned weakly against the door, hearing his Jaguar pull away and knowing in her heart that she was fighting not just him, but her own treacherous feelings as well.

# CHAPTER SEVEN

IN THE boutique on Monday Elin made the resolution to push aside her emotional turmoil and to concentrate on the business. Yet in between contacting her suppliers, attending to her customers and deciding which garments to put in the forthcoming sale, she continued to agonise.

Marriage to Roger had made her afraid of any form of commitment. And yet the idea of sharing her life with a man she was very strongly attracted to . . . of having his children one day . . . Wasn't the chance of happiness perhaps worth a risk?

Voicing her thoughts aloud, she said to Miriam during a lull in the afternoon when the shop was empty, 'Do you think I'm a very cautious person?'

'No, I wouldn't say you were cautious exactly,' Miriam said consideringly. 'More . . . level-headed. Why, what makes you ask?'

'You remember I mentioned meeting an old flame at the party I went to?' she said, going on as Miriam nodded, 'Well, yesterday he . . . he asked me to marry him.'

'My word, he certainly doesn't believe in letting the grass grow! I thought he looked a man of purpose when he was in the shop the other day.'

Startled, Elin said, 'How did you guess it was him?'

'It was just a hunch,' Miriam smiled. 'Plus your description of him. What was it you said—good-looking in a hard sort of way? I was sure it was him the moment

I saw you together.' She paused and then prompted, 'What did you say to him when he asked you to marry him—that you needed time to think about it?'

Elin shook her head.

'I told him no—for a number of reasons. But I'm sure it was the right answer.'

'Can you really put him out of your mind, just like that?' Miriam questioned.

'I'm determined to,' Elin said, 'because I'm not in love with him.'

Miriam gave her a thoughtful look, but made no attempt to contradict her statement. Instead, glancing at her watch, she said, 'It's almost half-past four, time for a cup of tea. I'll go and plug the kettle in.'

She had only just disappeared into the workroom when the shop bell jangled. Elin glanced up as the door opened wider and saw, to her utter dismay, that it was her ex-husband who had come into the boutique. It had taken him no time at all to locate her. She gripped the counter to steady herself, the shock and consternation she felt mirrored plainly on her face.

Her immediate impression was that he had changed little in the two years since they had been divorced. His brown hair still waved thickly and was worn rather long, curling over his forehead. In dark cords and an open-neck Western shirt he would have passed for a mature student rather than a university lecturer, even taking account for the fact that he was on holiday.

His blue eyes met hers without a qualm. Putting his hands into the pockets of his cords, he began cordially and with no trace of awkwardness, 'Hello, Elin. I expect your father tipped you off that I'm over here on vacation.'

Finding her voice at last, she managed, 'How did

you find me? I know my father didn't tell you.'

'No, he wasn't any too pleased when I called to see him on Saturday evening,' Roger said drily. 'Your friends closed ranks too. You must have really made out I was a monster.'

'I never discussed our marriage with anyone except my father,' she answered. 'If my friends wouldn't tell you my address it was because they guessed that, if I'd wanted you to have it, Dad would have given it to you.'

'Well, luckily one of them let slip you were running a boutique in Pinner. With "E.H. Fashions" on the door, I guessed this was the one.' He looked about him as he commented, 'It's very impressive. Do you run it alone?'

She recognised the combination of charm and relaxed ease that he had always been able to switch on so effortlessly.

'I have an assistant,' she replied, very glad at that moment of Miriam's presence. 'She's in the workroom, but she'll be out in a minute.'

'That's good,' he said. 'It means she can hold the fort for you while we go and have tea together somewhere. I noticed a tea-shop a little further down the high street on the other side of the road. Shall we go there?'

The shock of seeing him again was slowly receding. Feeling more able to cope, she said, 'I have customers to serve. I can't leave the boutique.'

'You just told me you have an assistant. You're not busy at the moment, and it's nearly closing time. Surely she can take over for the last half-hour or so?' Then, when his words seemed to be having no effect on her, he added impatiently, 'Look, all I want is to talk to you.'

She hesitated. She didn't want to get into a match of words with him in the boutique. It would damage trade if a customer walked in while they were arguing. Quickly she reasoned that she wouldn't be alone with him in the tea-shop.

'All right,' she conceded reluctantly. 'I'll just tell Miriam I'm going out.'

She went through into the workroom with its mahogany desk for doing the accounts and matching swivel-chair. Miriam was dipping a biscuit in her tea.

'I didn't pour yours because I heard the shop bell and guessed you had a customer,' she began.

'It wasn't a customer,' Elin said soberly. 'It's my ex-husband who's just walked in.'

'Your ex-husband?' Miriam echoed in surprise. 'Oh, heavens!'

'Yes, oh, heavens!' Elin murmured.

'Is he still here?'

'Yes. He's virtually insisted I go out for a cup of tea with him.'

'Are you sure that's wise?' Miriam said anxiously. 'I mean, you said he had a very volatile temper.'

'He hasn't been drinking and I don't think he'll want a row in public any more than I do. I'll be OK. If I go out with him it will probably be the quickest and easiest way of getting rid of him. I'll say goodbye to him at the tea-shop and then go straight home. Can I ask you to lock up for me?'

'Sure,' Miriam agreed. She set her mug of tea down. 'I'll take over from you straight away.'

Left alone in the workroom, and needing a few minutes' grace to steel herself for what lay ahead, Elin touched up her lipstick and neatened her hair. Looking in the mirror, she saw that her appearance gave no indication of how tense and wary she felt.

Suddenly Garel's words flashed into her mind. He was too astute, she thought turbulently. He'd guessed rightly when he'd said that beneath the façade there was a scared little cat. It hadn't always been that way and it made her angry. Since her divorce she had begun slowly to rebuild her confidence and self-esteem. But she doubted she would ever master her dread of confrontation. Her instinct was always to flee, never, unless she was cornered, to stand and fight.

When she came out of the workroom Miriam was at the separates rail showing a customer a selection of blouses. She flashed Elin a look of support as she left the shop with Roger.

As they walked down the sloping high street, he remarked, 'After Canada, you really notice things like the old Norman church and the half-timbered buildings. I didn't realise Pinner was so picturesque.'

'It's got a lot of charm,' she agreed, 'but then, in a completely different way, so has Vancouver. There's so much space in Canada.'

'Do you miss that?' he asked.

'I did for a while when I first came home.'

Stepping smartly off the kerb, she managed to avoid the touch of his hand at her elbow as they crossed the road. He opened the door of the black and white timbered tea-rooms and stood back for her to enter ahead of him.

The shop wasn't crowded, and she led the way to a table near the window that overlooked the street. The setting, with its exposed beams and brickwork, dark oak tables and window-boxes that were a mass of colour, was pleasant, calm and civilised. It reassured her. They couldn't get into much of an argument here.

A waitress in a black dress and crisp white apron quickly came to take their order.

'What would you like?' Roger asked Elin.

'Earl Grey tea with lemon.'

'And we'll have scones and strawberry jam as well,' Roger said as he glanced up at the waitress.

The girl moved away, and he sat back in his seat studying Elin for a moment or two before commenting, 'You're looking very well.'

'Thank you. So are you.'

'How long have you been running your own business?' he enquired.

'About two years,' she answered, her nerves tensing with the stilted conversation, and with wondering where it was leading to.

'It looks as if you're being very successful,' he remarked.

'I've got a good position in the high street, and designer clothes sell well round here,' she said before asking, 'And how are things with you?'

'I can't complain,' he replied. 'I've moved out of the apartment now and bought a house on Marine Drive.'

'Very nice,' she commented.

'I always said it was the place to live, overlooking the ocean.'

The tray came with its stainless steel teapot and hot-water jug. Elin poured out and then passed him his cup. She watched him warily as he began to butter a scone.

She had been wrong in thinking he hadn't changed. In repose his mouth had more of a sullen curve than she had remembered. The frown lines between his eyes were deeper.

'This reminds me of when we were dating,' he mused. 'Do you remember how we'd drive to the coast and then stop off at some tea-shop or other on the way back?'

'Yes, I remember,' she said tonelessly, thinking how naïve she'd been then, impressed by his brand of charm and his stimulating conversation.

There was a pause and then he said, lowering his voice to a more intimate tone, 'I miss you, Elin.' She didn't answer and he went on, 'I've given up drinking completely. I haven't touched a drop since——'

'Roger, please,' she interjected.

'No, let me go on,' he insisted. 'I've changed, Elin. I know I gave you a rough time when we were married. I know I hurt you, but I'm not like that any more. That's why I've come over here on holiday. I want us to get back together again.'

'You . . . you can't be serious!'

'I'm perfectly serious. I want you to come back with me to Vancouver in September.'

'Roger, we're divorced!'

'Do you think some damn piece of paper alters anything?' he countered fiercely. 'You're still my wife.'

'You're being ridiculous!'

His jaw clenched as he curbed his temper at her emphatic reply. 'We had some good times together, you and I,' he said. 'It could be like that again.'

'I still have the scars left from our marriage,' she reminded him, her throat tight.

He brought his fist down on the table, making the teacups rattle, and instinctively she flinched.

'I've told you. I've changed,' he repeated.

'And so have I,' she flared. 'And I'm not going to

be intimidated by you any more!'

'You just can't forgive me, can you?' he said bitterly. 'I forgave *you* when you broke off our engagement, but you can't forgive *me*.'

'I forgave you time and time again,' she countered.

'Then why can't you believe me when I tell you that this time things will be different?' he demanded.

'Because I've heard your promises before.'

'But now I mean to keep them.'

'Like the promises you made in church when we were married?' she asked, her eyes beginning to smart.

'You made promises, too, remember,' he shot back. 'Forever being one of them.'

'And it would have been forever if you hadn't made it impossible for me!' Her voice caught, and she paused to steady it before saying, 'I'm not coming back to Canada with you, Roger. I'm happy with my life here.'

His blue eyes pinned her. 'You've met someone else,' he said accusingly.

'I'm not involved with anyone,' she denied.

'You're lying!'

'Why should I lie to you? Look, can't you see this conversation is pointless? I'm sorry, Roger, but I don't love you any more.'

'You did once,' he reminded her.

'Yes, I did,' she agreed on a wry note.

'Are you saying I killed your love?' he demanded, raising his voice to her.

'Roger, please,' she said in an undertone. 'People are looking.'

'I don't care——' he began. Then, breaking off, he drew a deep breath and said, moderating his tone with an effort, 'I didn't ask you here to shout at you. I came to tell you that I still need you, that I still——'

'No, you don't,' she interrupted impatiently.

'I think I know better than you do what my feelings are,' he contradicted her with curbed force.

There was a short loaded silence, and then he commented tersely, 'You haven't touched your scone.'

'I'm not hungry.'

He reached across the table to take hold of her hand. She promptly withdrew it, and he asked angrily, 'Why won't you listen to me? We had something good——'

'A long time ago,' she cut in, sweeping on, 'I don't know why you're saying these things to me. You tell me you still need me, but it's been two years since we were divorced. Why, suddenly, have you decided you want me back?'

His mouth tightened, but he conceded, 'OK, I'll be honest about it. I was living with someone. Now it's broken up.'

'Has it?' she muttered.

'Aren't you curious to know why?'

'I think I can guess,' she said drily.

'Well, you're wrong,' he snapped. 'It broke up because she wasn't you.' He seemed about to say more, but checked himself. Leaning an elbow on the table, he rubbed the back of his neck with his hand. 'This is hopeless,' he declared with an angry sigh. 'I can't talk to you here. Can't we go back to your place?'

'There's no point,' she answered. 'You've said you want to try again, and I've said I'm not interested. There's nothing to be gained by going over it any longer. You won't change my mind.'

With that she got to her feet. As she went to walk past him, Roger caught hold of her by the arm and said, 'Wait till I've paid the bill.'

His insistence that she remain with him meant that

they finally parted outside the tea-shop. Meaning to make it clear to him that she was saying goodbye, she stated, 'I hope you enjoy your holiday over here. Have a safe journey back in September.'

His mouth twisted bitterly. 'It's been a long way to come for such a cold reception.'

Without answering him, she walked off. At the top of the high street she paused and, under the pretext of looking in the chemist's window, watched as Roger strode away in the opposite direction. Not till she had seen him round the corner did she set off home.

'Was it all right yesterday?' Miriam asked the following morning.

'Roger wanted a reconciliation,' she answered. 'I told him it was too late. He seemed to accept it. I don't think I'll see him again.'

But she was wrong. She got home that evening, showered, and changed into a denim skirt and short-sleeved cotton blouse. She hadn't heard from Garel since the weekend. As she prepared a meal for herself she wondered if he would ring her that evening, and was tempted to take the phone off the hook. Coming into contact with her ex-husband again had not only shaken her, it had made her value her freedom more than ever.

And yet her heart gave a leap of expectation when there was a sharp rapping at the door. Then she remembered the charity envelope that had been left a few days before and realised it must be someone calling to collect it. Garel would have rung the bell as he had on Sunday.

Getting to her feet, she went into the hall, picking up the envelope off the radiator shelf. She opened the door, incredulity swiftly followed by a surge of anger as she saw who the caller was. Acting on impulse, she made to slam the door shut, but Roger promptly thrust his foot inside the hall. He sent the door swinging back on its hinges, leaving her with no option but to retreat.

'What are you doing here?' she managed, her heart thumping and her mouth suddenly dry. 'How did you find out where I live?'

'Simple,' he shrugged. 'I followed you yesterday from the tea-shop.'

'But . . .' she faltered.

'Yes, I know,' he said sardonically, kicking the door to behind him. 'You were very careful to watch me till I'd rounded the corner before you set off home.'

'Have . . . have you been drinking?' she asked as she edged away from him.'

'You don't listen to anything, do you?' he said impatiently. 'I've told you—I don't drink any more. I'm stone-cold sober and, now that you've had the chance to get used to the idea that I want you back, I've come to talk to you again.'

There was no point in demanding that he leave. She knew she'd be wasting her breath. Desperately trying to work out a strategy to deal with the situation, she turned to go back into the lounge.

He followed her, glancing around him appreciatively before complimenting her, 'With the boutique and this house you've done very well for yourself in the last two years.'

She watched as he made himself at home on the sofa, and then said inventively, 'You can't stay. I'm expecting someone.'

His gaze flickered over her, taking in the denim skirt that moulded her slender hips, her casual blouse and her silky hair that was twisted into a simple knot.

'It doesn't look as though you are,' he replied.

She glared at him, and then crossed over to the phone and picked up the receiver.

'If you don't leave immediately,' she warned, 'I'm calling the police.'

He came towards her and pulled the receiver roughly out of her hand, slamming it back on its cradle.

'To tell them what?' he demanded. 'Am I threatening you? Am I harming you in any way?'

'Get out,' she said, without raising her voice, as she struggled to keep her fear in check.

'Now look,' he snapped, 'I've travelled some six thousand miles to see you. The least you can do in return is to be a little more welcoming.'

Anger was beginning to burn in his blue eyes and she took a step back from him. Wiping her clammy palms along the seams of her skirt, she forced herself to stay calm. She was trapped with him. The only way to forestall a fight was to play it cool and keep all her wits about her.

With great reluctance, she asked, 'Would . . . would you like a cup of coffee, then?'

'That sounds a little warmer,' he said approvingly. 'Thanks, I would.'

She went into the kitchen, spooned instant coffee into two cups, and added milk as she waited for the kettle to boil. Her thoughts were agitated. He wasn't drunk, she reminded herself, trying to steady her nerves, and she knew better than to arouse his temper. There was no reason to suppose that things were going to get out of hand.

His voice from the doorway startled her. Leaning against the frame, he asked, 'Were you being honest with me yesterday when you said you weren't involved with anyone?'

'Yes, I was,' she said tersely, pouring boiling water into the cups.

She went to pick up the tray, but he stopped her. 'Let me carry that for you,' he said.

He took it into the lounge where he set it down on the coffee-table. She waited until he was seated before choosing an armchair well away from him. Intending to direct the conversation so that there was no chance of its getting on to dangerous ground, she asked. 'How's your research work going these days?'

He had never needed much prompting to talk about his research, though he'd always been skilled at making it sound obscure. She listened to him with a pretence of interest while her gaze strayed periodically to the clock on the mantelpiece.

Half an hour went by while they talked, then another fifteen minutes. She could feel a headache coming on as she began to despair of getting him to go. The garden was retreating in the twilight. Normally she would have crossed over to the french windows to draw the curtains. Now she left them open. She had no intention of making the atmosphere seem cosy.

'I see you have a piano,' Roger remarked, getting to his feet to strike a couple of notes on it. 'I've still got the one I bought for you shortly after we were married. It's not been played since you left.'

'You might as well sell it,' she said unthinkingly, and immediately regretted her incautious reply.

She had finished her coffee some while ago and, feeling on edge with him so near to her, she stood up to replace her cup on the tray. Instead of returning to her chair, she sat down across the room from him on the sofa.

'I've no intention of selling it,' he said, glancing at her with a frown. 'It belongs to you just as you belong to me.'

Her heartbeat quickened uneasily, but she kept her voice quiet and firm as she said, 'Roger, you have to accept it: things are over between us.'

He came and sat down on the sofa beside her. Running a finger up her arm to the short sleeve of her blouse, he said softly, 'If that was true, my darling wife, you'd be involved with someone else by now.'

'Stop it,' she insisted, hunching her shoulder against his attempt to press a kiss against the hollow of her throat. 'And don't call me your darling wife!'

Roger laughed at her outburst, pressing her back against the sofa as she tried to get to her feet.

'Maybe it's time I kissed you properly to remind you of the old times.'

Suddenly, despite all her efforts, it was too late for stratagems.

'No!' she protested in alarm, turning her head away.

But immediately he snatched hold of her chin with bruising fingers, intent on making her submit to him. She closed her lips tightly as his mouth covered hers.

Fright and anger rose up inside her, making her struggle all the more wildly. Roger's lips ground against her teeth and she gave a muffled cry of pain. She thudded her fist against his shoulder in protest.

'You're my wife, damn it,' he muttered furiously, snatching hold of her wrist. 'I've never used force on you before, but, so help me, that's the way I'm going to take you if you won't co-operate.'

Terrified by his words, for a frozen instant she stared into his glittering eyes. The next she was fighting him with every ounce of strength she possessed. She heard a loud rip as the material of her blouse tore at the shoulder seam. Revulsion threatened to choke her as his hands fumbled for her breasts. Freeing her arm from the weight of his chest, she hit out blindly at him, her fingers raking across his face.

With a muttered oath he raised his head, cupping his hand to his scratched cheek. He glanced at his fingers, rage distorting his features as he saw the smear of blood on them. Lifting his hand, he slapped her deliberately across the face in retaliation. She cried out as the force of the blow jerked her head sideways.

He grabbed hold of her again and in her frenzy she heard the ringing of the doorbell. To summon help was her last chance, her only chance. Desperation urged her to an elemental action of self-defence. Sinking her teeth into his shoulder, she brought her knee up. Roger yelped and, in that moment, she managed to twist herself out of his grasp. She tumbled on to the floor, picking herself up so quickly that she wasn't even aware that the fall had jarred her. Roger made an angry grab for her, but missed.

He was close behind her as she fled into the hall. Gaining the front door, she snatched hold of the knob, succeeding in turning it before Roger caught up with her. His fingers twisted brutally in her hair as he dragged her back, and she screamed his name in protest.

Simultaneously Garel sent the door crashing back on its hinges as he strode into the hall. He assessed the situation in an instant, fury tightening his jaw, menace leaping like a raw flame in his dark eyes.

'Take your hands off her,' he ground out.

Crumbling at the threat of violence, Roger let his grip on her slacken, enabling her to tear herself free.

His gaze strayed to her angrily before he fired back at Garel, 'I don't know who you are, but you stay out of this. I'm her husband.'

'Not any more, you're not,' Garel growled, snatching hold of him by the lapels.

Overwhelmed with relief Elin sagged against the wall, her eyes closed, her face ashen, hardly daring to believe that the terrifying ordeal was over.

The next instant a harsh grunt had her eyes flying open in time to see Roger reeling back. Garel caught hold of him again, his hand still clenched into a fist. Knowing that she was safe, and that in another moment Garel would have thrown him out, she staggered into the lounge.

Going over to the drinks cabinet, with shaking hands she poured herself some brandy. She put the glass to her lips, her breathing coming in short, rasping gasps that meant she had to pause before she was able to swallow any of it. When she did, the fiery liquid burned her throat, making her eyes sting. She waited till the fit of coughing subsided and then raised the glass again. She took another sip, feeling the brandy's warmth stealing along her veins, bringing a measure of strength coursing back into her body.

The front door banged and, hearing a man's tread on the threshold, she whirled round, instinctive terror momentarily returning. Then, seeing Garel, she drew a sharp calming breath.

'Has . . . has he gone?' she asked in a barely audible whisper.

Garel strode towards her. He took hold of her by the shoulders, his face grimmer than she had ever seen it.

'What did he do to you?' he demanded.

She gazed up at him, too shaken to understand the

glitter in his eyes. She only knew that she had never heard him sound so quiet and yet so savage.

'N . . . nothing,' she stammered. 'I'm . . . I'm all right.'

'Nothing?' he repeated, a nerve jumping in his cheek. 'Your blouse is ripped, your face is badly bruised and you're shaking like a leaf. Now, what did he do?'

'He . . . he tried to . . . to make love to me. You . . . you came just in time. If you hadn't . . .'

As she spoke some of the tautness went out of his face. 'Thank God,' he muttered.

Taking the brandy glass from her, he set it aside, enfolding her tightly in his arms. She clung to him. She wanted to cry, but somehow the numbness and agony went too deep, and the sobs wouldn't come.

After a time she stopped trembling. Much as she wanted to stay in the haven of his arms, she drew away. As she did so she realised suddenly how badly her blouse was ripped. She blushed, and hurriedly brought a torn edge of the material up to cover the swell of her breast.

In a slightly cramped voice, she said, 'I'd better go and change my blouse.'

Garel studied her, a thoughtful light in his dark eyes as he scanned her features.

'I was wrong about you the other day,' he mused quietly. 'When it comes to a crisis, you're a lot tougher than I thought.'

There were several answers she might have made. Any one of them would have explained her state of numbed fortitude in the aftermath of what had happened. But she didn't say she was used to Roger's violent temper. Instead, the shiver that went through her as she thought of what Garel had saved her from made her deny huskily, 'I'm not tough—just . . . just very thankful that you called when you did.'

In the bedroom, feeling soiled from Roger's touch, she discarded not only her torn blouse but her skirt as well. She had changed into a dress and was sitting on the bed, her temples throbbing, when Garel came in.

Sweeping her hair away from her face, he pressed a cold, wet towel to the ugly bruise along her jaw, making her wince slightly. A curious ache tightened around her heart as she submitted in silence to his strong, caring hands.

'Is this the first time you've seen your ex-husband since your divorce?' he asked.

'He's been in Canada until now,' she said, her voice a whisper.

'Yet you asked him in and offered him coffee.'

His clipped tone made her dart a glance at his face. Seeing that his expression was hard and set, she flared without warning, 'That's right! Blame the victim. I gave Roger a cup of coffee so I deserved to be raped!'

'For God's sake,' he fired back. 'I'm just trying to understand what happened here this evening.'

'What happened——' she began stormily, and then broke off as to her consternation her vision blurred with tears.

With a smothered exclamation Garel gathered her into his arms. She resisted him briefly and then, as his hand came to rest against the back of her head, holding her to him protectively, she gave in to a deluge of tears. Unable to fight the sobs that racked her, she pressed her cheek against his shoulder, her fingers closing on a fistful of his shirt.

Garel pressed his lips against her temple.

'Elin, sweetheart, don't,' he murmured in a tortured tone. 'I can't bear to see you cry like this. I'm only angry because you're hurt.'

It took her some while to steady. His hand travelled in a caress over her shoulders that moved irregularly with her disturbed breathing. In a thin voice that was muffled by his shirt, she said, 'R-Roger forced his way in. I g-gave him coffee to appease him. I just wanted him to leave.'

She heard him swear softly and raised her head, not understanding the look of self-contempt she saw on his face.

'What . . . what is it?' she asked, brushing the tears from her cheeks with unsteady fingers.

'I was thinking how after James's party I invited myself in. Suddenly I'm not very proud of the way I intimidated you that night.'

'I did feel threatened,' she admitted in a whisper.

'Are you still afraid of me?' he demanded quietly, tilting her chin up towards him.

She shook her head imperceptibly. The honesty of her mute reply was perfectly apparent, and a glimmer of a smile softened his chiselled features. It was a fragile moment, and strangely precious.

Yet as he looked down into her tear-misted eyes the poignancy of it underwent a change. His gaze slipped to the curve of her mouth and her heart seemed to skip a beat. Tension gripped her, electric and sensual. Her lips parted as he combed his fingers deep into her hair.

Then suddenly she was free. Before she could pull her dazed senses together Garel was on his feet. Bewildered, she clutched at his sleeve as he turned towards the door.

'Don't go,' she pleaded in alarm. 'I'm . . . I'm scared

to be alone. Can't you stay and talk to me a little longer?'

'Do you think if I stay we're going to talk?' he asked bluntly.

She coloured and promptly let go of his arm. The thought of his leaving brought the image of Roger back into her mind, the fury she had seen in his eyes making her shiver.

'I . . . I just don't want to be in the house alone,' she appealed in a cramped voice. 'Not after what's happened.'

He breathed in deeply. His jawline was tight as he took in her pale, anxious face. With a short sigh of resignation he said gently, 'Get ready for bed, and I'll fix you some hot milk and brandy to help you go to sleep.'

# CHAPTER EIGHT

THE sound of her bedroom door opening woke Elin the next morning. She lifted her head from the pillow, pushing back her tumbled hair to see Garel, tall and arrestingly male, advancing into the room, a cup in his hand.

Still muddled from sleep, for an instant she blinked at him, noting his roughly hewn jaw and chin that were shadowed by a night's growth of beard. And then the events of the previous evening came rushing back and she sat up.

As she did so, Garel's gaze travelled to the smooth curve of her bare shoulders and her small breasts that were provocatively concealed by the cream and lace silk nightgown she was wearing. Her hands reached defensively for the covers, pulling them higher.

His astute dark eyes noted the instinctive reaction with sardonic amusement.

'Last night you fell asleep in my arms,' he mocked gently. 'Yet this morning you're shy with me.'

To her discomfort her memory chose that moment to remind her of how she had snuggled against the hard plane of his chest. Had she really slipped her hand inside his shirt to savour the solid warmth of him? Or had she dreamed it?

'You must have been very liberal with the brandy you put in the hot milk you gave me,' she said. 'I don't remember anything very clearly after drinking it.'

A wicked gleam came into his eyes. 'Are you asking

me to put your mind at rest?' he enquired blandly.

'No. I'm sure you . . . I mean . . .' She trailed off in blushing confusion.

The amused grooves in his tanned cheeks deepened.

'Relax, Elin,' he said. 'Despite what was on offer last night, I didn't serve myself. Now drink your tea.'

She took the cup from him, wishing she dared meet the directness of his eyes, and sorely tempted to flare up with him over his egotistical assumption. It was the knowledge of how much she owed him, coupled with the honesty that lay at the core of her nature, which stopped her.

Wanting to change the subject, she asked, 'What time is it?'

'Just after seven,' he answered. 'Would you like the curtains drawn back?'

'Please,' she answered, watching as he strode over to the window. Quickly she reached for her wrap that lay across the bed and pulled it on. Feeling slightly less vulnerable, she asked as the swish of the curtains brought the sunlight spilling into the room, 'Where did you sleep?'

'Downstairs on the sofa. I found a couple of blankets in the cupboard on the landing.'

'It . . . it was very nice of you to sleep here. I haven't thanked you yet for what you did.'

'How are you feeling?'

'I'm fine,' she said, and then added as the least she could do to express her gratitude, 'Will you stay for breakfast? I've got bacon and eggs in the fridge, and it won't take me a minute to shower and dress.'

'Sounds good,' he said, a sensual note in his voice. 'I'm hungry.'

When she joined him in the kitchen a short while

later he was leaning with his back against the worktop, glancing through the financial section of *The Times*. He set the paper aside on seeing her.

He might have spent an uncomfortable night cramped on her sofa, but, apart from the fact that he needed a shave, he gave little sign on it. With his arms folded across his chest he looked as alert and as predatory as ever, his presence dominating the kitchen.

Hardening her heart against his dark good looks and virility, she moved past him to light the grill.

'What's the news this morning?' she asked.

'The stock market went up a couple of points yesterday, but it looks as if the bank rate will have to rise again, which isn't so good.'

'At least it will keep inflation in check,' she remarked.

'I didn't know you followed the economy with such interest.'

She glanced at him, suspicious from his comment that he had guessed she was trying to subdue her awareness of him by keeping the conversation impersonal. But his face was impassive and, reassured, she answered, 'Running my own business, I have to.'

They chatted about various topics as they ate. It felt strangely right to be sitting opposite him over breakfast. She found herself studying his face, the aggressive thrust of his jaw, the faint lines at the corners of his eyes that crinkled when he smiled, his hard, sensual mouth.

Her heart contracted oddly and, as it did so, her gaze inadvertently met his. A flicker of electricity travelled along her nerves like a warning. As so often between them, the atmosphere suddenly held too much static. She would have made some attempt to damp it down had he not remarked first, 'To share breakfast with a woman, but not her bed, is something of a novelty.'

She got to her feet and carried their plates over to the sink.

'It's a little early in the morning for innuendoes of that kind,' she said shortly.

She heard the sound of his chair being pushed back.

'I unsettle you, don't I?' he mocked.

'Not in any way,' she lied.

She bent to put the milk jug in the fridge. As she straightened up she collided with his hard body. Shying away defensively, she snapped, 'Do you have to stand on top of me?'

His dark brows came together, his eyes hard and steady on her face.

'Why don't you stop behaving so skittishly and admit to yourself you're attracted to me?' he demanded.

'Perhaps I am attracted to you,' she admitted, 'but that doesn't mean I can't live without you!'

'Really?' he murmured.

'Yes, really,' she insisted, her temper flaring as she saw the scepticism on his swarthy face. 'I'm a reasonably capable, reasonably enterprising woman and, much as I'm grateful to you for staying with me last night, in general I can manage my life very adequately. I don't need any help from you!'

He reached out and pulled her against his chest, his arms sliding around her waist to hold her captive.

'You're a regular spitfire this morning,' he laughed huskily. 'It's been a stormy courtship. It looks as if it's going to be a stormy marriage.'

'And *who* says I'm going to marry you?' she demanded, wedging a breathing space between them with her elbows.

'I do,' he returned. 'For the simple reason, my green-eyed witch, that you want me as much as I want you.'

Her eyes sparked as she glared at him, his intimate words quickening her pulse and fanning her temper.

'I've admitted that I'm attracted to you physically,' she said turbulently, 'but even if I were to get married again, I wouldn't choose someone like you! I get the impression there has been a series of women in your life over the last few years and——'

'I'm quite prepared to settle for one woman,' he cut in, adding lazily, 'Unless, that is, you think you can't satisfy me, though from what I remember——'

'Stop it!' she hissed, trying to push his hands from her waist.

'Stop what?' he asked as he freed her. 'All I'm doing is talking to you. Last night you said that was what you wanted. Or this morning were you hoping for a little action rather than a discussion about our relationship?'

'All I'm hoping is that you'll get the message I'm trying to spell out. You're not what I need, Garel.'

His gaze narrowed slightly as it held hers, a depth of masculine knowledge in his dark eyes.

'I wonder,' he mused.

It alarmed her to discover a similar doubt deep down in herself, a doubt that made her flare with all the more emphasis, 'There's no wondering about it! You're a law unto yourself, impossible to handle, and you remind me too much of . . .'

'Go on,' he prompted. 'I've no objection to your being frank.'

'All right, then. At times you remind me of a wolf on the prowl.'

'So tame me.'

Her heart seemed to skip a beat, a warm shiver tracing over her skin at his softly spoken challenge.

'I don't want to tame anyone,' she insisted. 'What I want is a partner, someone understanding, someone loyal and affectionate, a man who'd be not just my lover, but my friend as well.'

'I thought you said you liked being single,' Garel mocked.

Angrily she realised that he had flustered her to the point where she had given away a secret wish that hitherto she had denied even to herself. He saw the tinge of betraying colour that crept into her cheeks and went on curtly, 'Let me give you some advice, Elin. Stay unattached before you choose a husband with the qualities you've just listed.'

'What's wrong with those qualities?' she flashed back.

Ironically, she had recently discovered many of them in him.

'You're too spirited a woman to want some doormat of a man,' he returned. 'If all you're looking for is loyalty and affection, buy yourself a dog.' He glanced at his watch. 'And now I have to be leaving for work.'

She mastered her annoyance at his words, remembering how greatly she was in his debt, and went with him to the front door to see him out. It was as he was about to leave that a thought suddenly struck her, and she caught hold of him by the arm.

'Garel, you don't think . . .' she faltered.

'I don't think what?'

'That Roger will come back.'

'I'd be very surprised after the lesson I gave him,'

Garel said grimly. He bent to graze her temple lightly with his lips. 'Goodbye, Elin.'

She stood with her hand against the door-frame, her thoughts agitated as he strode off down the drive. Was this a casual parting, or was Garel walking out of her life for good? He hadn't said he'd be in touch. He'd said goodbye. Did she honestly expect him to contact her again when she'd turned him down twice?

Gripped by indecision, she watched as he unlocked the door of his Jaguar, the sunlight burnishing his black hair. One minute she thought of her freedom; the next she remembered his strength and protectiveness the night before, the rapport she had felt with him over breakfast. She decided suddenly, so what if she'd always be second in his life to Carol? So what everything?

'Garel . . .' she called.

Her husky voice didn't carry and, desperate to stop him before he got into his car and pulled away, she sped down the drive and into the street. At the sound of her footsteps he turned, his brows drawing together as he saw her running towards him.

Catching him up, she began in a breathless rush, for once letting herself be ruled by emotion and not her head, 'Garel . . . I . . . I've changed my mind. I . . . I'll marry you!'

Something leapt in the depths of his dark eyes. Combing his hands into her hair, he muttered, 'Sometimes I wonder if I'll ever fathom you, but right now I don't give a damn.'

Her heart fluttered as he bent his head to claim her mouth. Drawing her closer, he crushed her against him, kissing her softly at first as though mindful of her ordeal the night before, and then, as her arms wound tightly around his neck, with a swift gradation of intensity that had her whole body on fire with dizzy longing.

When his dark head finally lifted, he looked down at her with shuttered eyes that concealed the smoulder of desire. Tracing the smoothness of her cheek with a caressing finger, he murmured, 'We're not having a long engagement, sweetheart. You've got just three weeks to get ready for our wedding.'

'Three weeks?' she echoed in protest. 'Garel, I can't——'

His mouth came down to silence her with a swift, gentle kiss.

'You can,' he said.

His prediction proved to be correct. The next weekend she had his emerald engagement ring on her finger, and less than three weeks later his wedding-ring joined it. As the chauffeur-driven white BMW sped them away from the Register Office to the old coaching inn where their reception was being held, Garel asked, 'Feeling better now it's over?'

'Was it obvious that I was nervous?' she asked.

'Was that all it was, just nerves?'

'What else? It . . . it was quite a step.'

'I'm glad your courage didn't fail,' he said, drawing her hand possessively through his arm.

'It nearly did when James took a minute to find the ring,' she said with the ghost of a laugh. She leaned her head against his shoulder. 'What would you have done if I'd tried to back out?'

'Put you across my knee and spanked you, I expect,' he said humorously.

She stiffened and drew away, studying the gold band on her finger that now bound her to him for better or for worse.

'What's wrong?' he demanded.

'I don't find jokes like that funny.'

'You really are on edge, aren't you?' he said, a slight shading of impatience in his voice. 'You need a drink to unwind.'

The laughter and light-heartedness of the reception made her relax and forget the brief twist of unease she had felt. Garel's dark eyes met hers as, following the speeches, they cut the cake together, his capable hand covering hers. She smiled at him, the look that flashed between them making her certain that their marriage was going to be a strong and happy one.

It seemed no time after that before they were being showered with confetti and good wishes as they got into Garel's Jaguar for the drive to Heathrow. Elin turned to wave goodbye to her father and to the group of friends who stood clustered in the inn's courtyard to see them off.

As they picked up the motorway, Garel remarked with a smile, 'You've got confetti in your hair.'

She laughed and reached up her hand to her chignon.

'And you're still wearing your carnation,' she said teasingly. 'Everyone will know we're a honeymoon couple.'

'They will at the hotel,' he agreed, reaching for her hand and drawing it across his leg to rest on his hard thigh. 'I've ordered flowers and champagne to be put in our room.'

He caressed her hand with his thumb as though to persuade her to leave it where he had placed it before his own returned to the wheel.

'What time did you say we arrive in Tenerife?' she

queried, hoping her voice didn't sound as husky to him as it did to her.

He slanted a glance at her, leashed desire in his eyes as he teased gently, 'Impatient to get there?'

A flush of colour in her cheeks, she withdrew her hand and said defensively, 'I was just wondering how long the flight is.'

'You've no need to blush,' he smiled. 'There's nothing wrong in looking forward to something we both know is going to be very pleasurable.'

The hotel he had booked them into on the northern part of the island was luxurious, set in its own tropical gardens on a slight hill above Puerto de la Cruz. They were shown up to their room which had its own bathroom and terrace.

She wandered over to the french windows and pushed them open to admire the view of snow-capped Mount Teide in the distance. Garel came to stand behind her. His hands slid around her waist as he pulled her back against him. She closed her eyes, feeling his lips touch the nape of her neck.

'What are you thinking?' he murmured.

'That this morning we were two separate people and now we're united as one.'

'Not quite, we're not,' he said meaningfully.

He had been more tolerant regarding her refusal to sleep with him before they were married than she had expected. The issue had arisen the same day as their engagement. Garel had made no secret of how much he desired her, and the atmosphere that evening at his house had been quick to ignite into passion.

'Garel, stop it,' she had gasped. 'Please, I . . . I'm not ready for this.'

'You were good and ready a couple of minutes ago,'

he'd frowned. His eyes had considered her as he allowed her to free herself from his embrace, a puzzled light in their depths that an instant before had been aglitter with passion. 'What is it you're scared of, Elin?' he had demanded. 'Making a commitment to me?'

'I've made a commitment to you,' she'd reminded him shakily. 'I've promised to marry you.'

Her fingers had fumbled with the buttons of her blouse, fastening only two of them before he tilted her chin up.

'Yes, you have,' he'd said. 'So why are you so reluctant to let me make love to you?'

'I'm . . . I'm not reluctant,' she'd replied, her face hot. 'I just want to wait until after we're married.'

'That's a little unusual these days,' he'd said sceptically. 'Especially considering how you went to bed with me five years ago.'

'What happened that night doesn't mean I don't have certain moral values!' she had retorted.

His astute gaze had narrowed on her flushed face.

'So you want to wait till my wedding-ring's on your finger,' he'd summarised. 'That's the only reason.'

She couldn't have given him a fuller explanation even had she wanted to. Only days before, she had been adamant that she would never again surrender her emotional sovereignty to any man. Now things were moving so fast that it frightened her. She had nodded in answer to his question and he'd given a short sigh, the expression on his chiselled features indecipherable.

'Then you'll have to try not to tempt me too much,' he'd said, getting up from the sofa and going to pour himself a drink.

They had dinner at the hotel before, at her suggestion, going for a stroll in the floodlit grounds. The night air was heady with the perfume of the poinsettias, hibiscus and bougainvillaea which grew in rich profusion. Moonlight silvered the pathways that curved between the jacaranda trees.

On an ornamental bridge spanning a shallow lake Elin paused, placing both her hands on the wooden railing.

'Happy?' Garel asked quietly, his finger brushing a stray tendril of hair that lay on her neck.

'It's like paradise here,' she murmured.

A dance band was playing at the hotel, the haunting, romantic music carrying towards them. Closer at hand she could hear the sound of Garel's breathing, and her own that had quickened slightly as he drew her shoulders back against him.

His hands slid inside her thin silk blouse, stroking her warm skin. At once she closed her eyes, hit by vertigo and desire. Counting her racing heartbeats, Garel murmured, 'I think, *cariad*, we're both ready for bed.'

In their room she sat at the dressing-table in a revealing ice-blue nightgown, brushing her hair. Her gaze flickered to him as he came out of the bathroom, wearing a loosely belted robe, their eyes meeting in the mirror. She set the brush down, conscious of an exquisite tension as she waited for him to cross the room to her.

'That's a very seductive nightgown,' he murmured, sweeping aside her hair. He lowered his head to press his mouth against the curve of her neck and shoulders while sliding his hands down her arms. 'Did you buy it specially?'

Her heart thumping, she whispered, 'Yes.'

Garel smiled, something like triumph leaping into his eyes. He drew her to her feet and turned her into his arms. Her fingers slid up, clutching at his neck as the firmness of his mouth on hers sent a familiar hot, melting pleasure licking along her veins.

She shivered as his lips explored the smooth planes of her face before seeking the sensitive hollow of her throat. He lifted his head, seeing the hot glow in her eyes as her lashes flickered up. Immediately he slid the straps of her nightgown off her shoulders.

She gasped as it fell with a silken whisper to the floor and he laughed huskily, swinging her up into his arms to carry her to the bed. As he laid her on the mattress her hand reached out for the light, but he forestalled her.

'You're beautiful,' he said, his voice deep and not quite steady. 'Why hide such loveliness from me?'

His glittering gaze ran over her before he followed the path his eyes had taken with his mouth. Driven by a need of her own, she pushed his robe from his shoulders.

His body was tanned and hard, and she caressed his hot skin, her trembling fingers suddenly digging into his back as his tongue encircled her nipple. He slid his palms the whole length of her, bending across her to encircle her waist with kisses before finding her mouth again.

Aflame with desire, she arched against him, as responsive to his touch as a musical instrument in the hands of a master, an instrument that had forgotten the beauty of the notes which could be struck on it. Garel's lips adored her, leading her deeper and deeper into a labyrinth of pleasure. A shock of excitement went through her as his hand travelled up her inner thigh. He caressed her intimately, working up the fever in her to storm force.

'Now, Garel. Please, now!' she moaned, scarcely knowing what she was saying as she begged him to release her from a pleasure so frenzied and intense that it was almost more than she could bear.

'Kiss me first,' he demanded raggedly.

He touched her mouth with his as he moved to cover her. She opened her lips, and then broke the kiss with a cry of ecstasy as he thrust forward.

As the racing wildfire flamed hotter and hotter she clung to his sweat-dampened shoulders, raking her fingers down his spine as the crescendo gathered to explode in a blinding starburst of release. She felt Garel shudder against her, hearing his harsh groan of fulfilment as she tumbled into dizzy freedom.

It was a long time before she stirred, and then it was in response to his tender caress as she lay in his embrace.

'All right?' he asked her softly.

Enfolded in the afterbliss of their lovemaking, she murmured with a sigh, 'More than all right, drowsy and content and . . .'

'Satisfied?' he suggested, his voice deep and gently teasing.

He felt her smile against his chest and reached out to switch off the bedside lamp. His body was warm and protective as he held her close in the shadowy darkness. Tracing his hand up the curve of her slim back, he asked, 'How did you get the scars on your shoulder, *cariad?*'

His voice in the dark was tender and caressing, but at his question her eyes flickered wide open. She raised her head, her fingers going to cup her right shoulder-blade.

Seeing the sharp lights of pain in her eyes, Garel kissed her. 'I wouldn't have asked if I'd known you were sensitive about them,' he said gently, his hand stroking her waist. 'I only wondered what happened.'

She would have told him, had it not been that she wanted no shadow from the past to fall across a night of such magical unity. Temporising, she whispered, determined to forget, 'I'm accident-prone.'

'Then I'll have to take very good care of you.'

She smiled softly, nestling her head back under his chin. 'You just have,' she murmured.

Their fortnight's holiday was an idyll, the days and nights merging together like a golden dream. It was as if they were enclosed in a world of their own, oblivious to all else but their consuming passion for each other.

They went sightseeing, hiring a car to explore the island's mountainous interior, strolled through the old town with its elegant traditional architecture and open markets, and wandered along empty beaches with the waves lapping around their ankles. By the time they flew back to London Elin had discovered that her love for her husband was something that invaded and pervaded every waking and sleeping moment.

Back home they slipped into their new life together easily. She enjoyed adding some feminine touches to his house and expressing her own taste and personality. She made sure she consulted him before she altered anything, but he seemed quite happy to let her have a free hand.

She enjoyed entertaining, and Garel was appreciative of the trouble she went to whenever he asked business clients round for drinks or dinner. Yet, despite the many deeply satisfying moments they shared, their quiet midnight conversations, and the long-shared pleasure of their lovemaking, some vague element was missing in their marriage.

She tried to deny it, because she wanted to believe that Garel felt for her more than desire, that he loved her as well. It was the way he looked at her sometimes when he thought she was unaware which first made her wonder if he was comparing her with Carol.

Turning quickly, she frequently caught him watching her: When her brows came together questioningly his mouth would curve into a smile, and she would tell herself firmly that she had imagined it, that she had no reason to be jealous of his first wife when they were building a good marriage.

Ironically, it was her attempt to strengthen their relationship by being honest with him which caused the row that put a rift between them. They were having friends round for a dinner party one Saturday evening. Everything was well in hand in the kitchen, and the table with its crystal, silver and central flower arrangement looked lovely.

Garel, virile and urbane in a grey suit and white shirt, handed her a glass of sherry.

'You not only seem to manage the cooking effortlessly, but you always looks stunning as well,' he remarked, kissing her lightly, a sensual note in his charismatic voice. 'I'm very proud to have you as my wife.'

'And I'm very happy just being your wife,' she told him, straightening his patterned silk tie in a gesture that was more loving than necessary.

He claimed her mouth again, the kiss they

exchanged sweet and lingering and heady. As his hands pulled her zip lower she drew away from him.

'We've got visitors coming,' she protested with a husky laugh. He recaptured her before she'd had time to refasten her zip, and more firmly she said, 'Garel, stop it.'

'Is it the time factor, or the marks on your shoulder that mean you don't want me nuzzling your neck?' he asked.

He felt her stiffen under his hands. As he zipped her dress up for her she said in a voice that was suddenly a shade cramped, 'The scars don't worry me.'

He turned her to face him, taking her glass from her and setting it aside as he said gently, 'Then the memory of what caused them does. What happened, Elin?'

Her eyes darkening, she pushed at his arms and, watching her closely, he released her. He'd guessed accurately; the memories *were* painful, but she meant to have no secrets from him. Her voice tight, she said, 'You saw how violent Roger could be that night you threw him out of my house.'

A frown of incredulity crossed Garel's face before his jaw tightened.

'Are you saying . . .? Are you telling me your ex-husband scarred you like that?' he demanded, a fierce note in his voice.

She nodded and admitted quietly, 'I was what's commonly known as a battered wife.'

There was a short silence and then Garel said harshly, 'Well, that explains a lot.'

Her startled gaze flew to him. Whatever she had been expecting from him in response to her confession, it certainly wasn't the angry censure she heard in his voice and saw in his face.

She thought that she shared a close relationship with Garel. But as they sat at opposite ends of the dinner table laughing and talking with their friends despite what was simmering between them, she began to wonder bitterly how much else in their marriage was a sham.

When she had told her father about Roger's violent behaviour he had tempered his fury with his son-in-law, knowing that to hear a tirade against the man she was in the process of divorcing wasn't going to lessen her pain. Her father had been a bulwark of strength and understanding when she had returned home from Canada, having finally left Roger.

She realised she had hoped to receive a measure of that same compassion and understanding from Garel. A man who loved her would surely have reacted in much the same way as her father had done. The thought curled round her heart like a cold snake.

Their visitors stayed until late, still joking and chatting as the dinner party broke up. James was the last to leave. Garel talked to him for a while in the hall before seeing him out.

Elin heard the front door close and then Garel joined her in the kitchen.

'I'll see to stacking the dishwasher,' he offered. 'You look tired.'

'It won't take a minute,' she told him, adding, 'You don't need to stay. I can manage on my own.'

His jaw hardened imperceptibly as he studied her.

'OK, if you prefer it that way,' he agreed.

It was only because she knew him so well that she caught the slight edge of sarcasm in his voice. She watched as he strode out of the kitchen, her hand going to the tense muscles of her neck.

On the surface the tension between them seemed to have been defused by an evening with friends. The reality was different. She sensed that for some reason Garel was still displeased with her. Had she not felt so hurt and resentful of his attitude towards what she had told him earlier in the evening, she would have demanded to know why.

Garel was in bed reading when she came out of the en-suite bathroom, her beauty routine completed. She had deliberately spun out the last few tasks left in the kitchen, but he had made no comment on the fact that she was so late in coming upstairs.

Conscious of a darting pain in her temples, she slipped off her petticoat in silence and unfastened her bra. Her nightgown was lying on the bed and, eyes downcast, she picked it up. As she did so the prickling of her skin made her sense unmistakably Garel's gaze on her.

Immediately she jerked her head up to see that he had set his book aside and was watching her, the glitter of desire in his dark eyes. Their gaze locked for an instant before his eyes swept leisurely over her naked breasts and shoulders. Her breathing quickened with his raking masculine scrutiny.

'You can come to bed without your nightgown,' he said, his tone soft and yet, paradoxically, abrasive. 'You won't be needing it.'

'I've got a headache,' she answered tautly, dropping her nightgown swiftly over her head.

'That's not a very original excuse, *cariad*,' he mocked gratingly.

'It may not be,' she replied as she crossed over to the dressing-table where she began to unpin her hair. 'But it happens to be the truth.'

A strange anger was mounting inside her. She wanted to be more to Garel than a woman whose company he enjoyed and who pleased him sexually in bed. She wanted him to love her the way she loved him, wanted what she knew from the strength and forcefulness of his personality he had inside him to give to the right woman.

A hairpin slipped out of her fingers and tinkled to the floor. Garel observed her, his eyes sharp.

'You seem very on edge tonight,' he commented.

'I'm tired, that's all.'

'Then come to bed.'

'I'm not ready yet,' she answered.

She began to brush her silken hair. As she continued with the slow, rhythmic strokes her gaze flickered to him in the mirror. As she had suspected, he was still watching her with unnerving steadiness, the bedside lamp that sculpted his chiselled features in light and shadow making the lines of his face seem more saturnine.

She was aware of his leanly muscled chest, of the dark smudge of hair that ran down towards his loins, which were covered by the bedclothes. Hurriedly she looked away, her pulse quickening with the curious tension that was vibrating in the softly shadowed room.

She started perceptibly as a moment later he threw back the covers. Pulling on his robe, he came towards her, a predator's grace and silence in his tread. He looked very big when he stood so close, and she stopped brushing her hair. From the set of his jaw, his temper was simmering just as hers was, yet his voice was even as he said, 'A good massage works wonders for tense muscles and a headache.'

'So do a couple of aspirin,' she replied. 'I think there's a bottle in the bathroom cabinet.'

'I thought you enjoyed having me touch you,' he mocked softly, sliding his hands down her bare arms.

She didn't know whether it was his touch, or the harsh note she detected in his voice, which sent a shiver down her spine. But, reacting instinctively, she stood up and whirled to face him.

'When I'm in the mood,' she snapped in agreement. 'Which tonight I'm not!'

'That's too bad,' he fired back, 'because *I am*.'

She struck her fist against his shoulder as he swung her up into his arms. He carried her to the bed and dropped her on the coverlet. His knee rested on it as he towered above her, something primitive and conquering in his stance as he stripped off his robe and flung it aside.

'Let go of me,' she choked as his mouth came down on hers.

His kiss was merciless, a passionate, arrogant act of dominance and possession that made her feel plundered and invaded. She struggled to twist free from his hold.

'Garel, please . . .' she panted. 'No!'

'Then stop fighting me,' he muttered huskily.

'You're no different from Roger!' she sobbed.

The panic in her voice seemed to reach him. He raised his body a little from hers, his head lifting.

'What do you mean?' he growled, as he stared down into her face.

'My ex-husband tried to rape me too, remember?' she breathed.

For an instant his grip tightened. He held her rigid, his face tauter than she had ever seen it. Then suddenly, he released her, swinging his feet to the carpet. She heard him swear savagely under his breath. Raking a hand through his hair, he stood up and paced to the window, anger in every line of his strong, naked body.

Stifling a sob, she clutched hold of her wrap, the tightness in her throat threatening to strangle her. She dragged it on, her trembling legs almost giving way beneath her as she got up from the bed. Immediately he turned to demand roughly, 'Where are you going?'

'I'm sleeping in the guest room tonight,' she said in a cramped voice. She looked back at him from the doorway to add bitterly, 'I thought when I told you about Roger . . . It doesn't matter what I thought.'

# CHAPTER NINE

WHEN Elin woke it was just after nine. Her eyes burning with unshed tears, she had finally drifted off into an exhausted sleep in the early hours of the morning. She threw back the covers and got up.

She pulled on her wrap, remembering the occasions when Roger had vented the full force of his fury on her, and finding she was comparing their fights with the one that had erupted between her and Garel. She'd always told herself that her ex-husband's unpredictable temper was connected with his drinking. Now suddenly she wasn't so sure.

She had no idea what had been the exact cause of the flare-up between her and Garel, but whatever had prompted it, last night, despite his self-control, she'd sensed he'd been furious with her.

The house was quiet. On Sundays they generally slept in, and she assumed that Garel wasn't up yet. Her clothes were in the main bedroom. The thought of fetching them made a picture of him flash into her mind, his head dark against the pillow, the covers slipped low to reveal the hard muscles of his swarthy chest. Even when he was asleep, his virility was a potent dominating force.

She hesitated, unwilling to walk into the matrimonial bedroom. Her entry was bound to wake him, and she could imagine only too clearly his satirical gaze as he assessed her in the insubstantial blue silk wrap she had snatched up when she had fled from him the previous night. It was the resentment she felt towards him that stiffened her backbone.

Ignoring the slight fluttering of her pulse, she pushed open the door to their room. To her surprise it was empty, the curtains drawn back, sunlight falling in a wide rectangle across the fitted carpet. Her eyes went to the tangled covers on the bed. They suggested that Garel had slept little better than she had.

She crossed over to her wardrobe, dressing quickly in a blue and white cotton top and a pair of hip-hugging jeans. A hint of soft rose blusher on her cheekbones disguised her paleness.

She went downstairs, guessing from the aroma of freshly brewed coffee that Garel was in the kitchen. Steeling herself, she advanced to join him. His hard gaze swivelled to her as she paused in the doorway, his face impassive.

Like her, he was clad in jeans, which moulded the strong length of his thighs. His hair glistened after his shower, its raven thickness unruly in a sensual sort of way.

She had the notion that he was waiting for her to speak first, and with cold composure she began, 'Good morning. Have you cooked bacon and eggs for both of us?'

'You generally eat a cooked breakfast on Sunday,' he reminded her, his voice a shade curt.

'I'm not very hungry this morning,' she said, her tone matching his. 'Toast would have done.'

He appeared to check his next comment, merely pointing out reasonably as he set the plates down on the table, 'You don't have to eat it.'

She pulled out a chair and poured herself a glass of orange juice. Garel sat opposite her. She could sense his gaze on her. Hating the tension that lingered in the air after their row, she began buttering a piece of toast.

When, finally, she found something to say, it was to speak at the same time as he did. Immediately she broke off, but, despite the slight tightening of his jaw, he deferred to her, curbing whatever remark it was he had been about to make.

'Go on,' he prompted evenly.

'I was wondering if the newspaper's come yet.'

'It's on the worktop.'

'Good. I want to have a look later at the solution to last week's jumbo crossword. With your help I nearly got it finished.'

Garel's black brows came together in a frown.

'Let's dispense with the inconsequential chatter, shall we?' he suggested.

Stung by his rebuff, she said with a flash of hostility, 'If that's what you want.' She got to her feet. 'In which case I'll check the crossword now.'

His knife and fork clattered on to his plate.

'That wasn't what I meant,' he said, impatience roughening his deep voice.

'Then what did you mean?' she demanded.

'I meant that I wanted to talk about last night.'

As he spoke the cat flap banged and Sam came into the kitchen. With a little miaow he ran towards Elin on silent paws.

'Sam wants to be fed,' she said, turning to the fridge.

Angrily Garel pushed back his chair. He caught hold of her by the arm, spinning her round to face him.

'I'm *trying* to apologise,' he said grittily.

'Are you?' she flashed, hurt and confused. 'Well, saying sorry doesn't always make it right.'

'What do you want me to do? Go down on my

knees? I've apologised for being short-tempered with you——'

'An apology isn't good enough,' she interrupted. 'I want to know why you were angry with me, why you're still angry with me. Just what did I do? Was it because I had a headache and didn't want to make love?'

'Don't be so damned ridiculous!' he exploded.

'*Am* I being ridiculous?' Her voice none too steady, she rushed on, 'You can be ruthless when you want something. And you wanted me, didn't you? That's why you asked me to marry you. Does the fact that you want me mean that I have to allow you your marital rights whenever you want them, regardless of my feelings?'

'And just what are your feelings?' he asked sarcastically.

She loved him so much and, at that moment, she felt he loved her so little in return. It prompted her to spark, 'You wouldn't understand.'

He kept his hard gaze on her, a slightly bitter twist to his mouth. 'I understand, sweetheart, only too well,' he said harshly. 'You wanted someone to protect you from your ex-husband, and you picked me. I wondered why, when you'd kept stating you didn't want to get involved with me, you suddenly changed your mind that morning, and ran after me as I left your house to say you'd marry me. But it's perfectly clear now.'

'That's not true!' she protested. 'I——'

'Isn't it?' he cut in angrily. 'Why not admit it? You married me because you were afraid Roger might come back and molest you.'

'No, I didn't!' she flashed. 'I married you . . .' Her voice caught, choking off the words. His accusation

that she had married him for an ulterior motive hurt
her all the more deeply because she loved him so. The
pain she was feeling made her hiss at him, almost in
tears, 'What's the point? I'm not going to defend
myself to you.'

Her vision blurring, she went to brush past him, but
he caught hold of her by the arm.

'Elin . . .'

'Let go of me,' she demanded fiercely.

'Not till you finish what you were saying. Now tell
me. Why did you marry me if it wasn't because of
Roger?'

'Because I love you!' she said, the words wrenched
from her. 'Though for all you care . . .'

Her voice choked to a stop again.

'God, Elin, I'm sorry,' he muttered raggedly as he
pulled her into his arms. 'You were so elusive and so
adamant you wouldn't marry me, that when you told
me last night how you got those scars on your shoulder
it all seemed to fit.'

With his words all the fight went out of her.
Understanding now the reason for his anger, she slid
her arms around his waist.

'I said I'd marry you because I love you,' she
repeated in a whisper. 'I thought you were saying
goodbye forever that morning you walked out of my
house.'

'Then you underestimated my determination,' he
said, a shading of humour back in his voice as he tilted
her chin up. He frowned slightly. 'Sweetheart, you're
trembling.'

She attempted a smile. 'I can't help it,' she
murmured. 'I hate rows. They scare me.'

'Because of Roger?'

She nodded. 'He . . . he'd start shouting at me and then . . .'

Garel's jaw tightened as he drew her back into his embrace. His lips brushed her hair.

'I'd never hurt you, Elin,' he said in a husky voice that seemed to come straight from the depths of his heart. 'Never, sweetheart.'

'I know,' she whispered.

With the rift made up between them everything returned to normal. Now that Garel knew and understood what had happened between her and Roger, she felt even closer to him. His protectiveness warmed her, engendering in her a sense of security and confidence she'd almost forgotten.

While she enjoyed her work at the boutique, she was much prompter in leaving after it shut now that she was married. She liked being home in the evenings to welcome Garel when he came in, and she was sorry when he announced, a few days later, that he would be away until the weekend on a business trip.

The very first night he was away she missed him. She lay for a long while staring up at the darkened ceiling, wishing he slept beside her. They hadn't been married long, yet already she found herself thinking how much she wanted his child. It was a longing that made her ache for him. She wanted to lie wrapped in his arms, having conceived in a storm of tender and impassioned lovemaking.

Restlessly she dragged the pillow more comfortably under her cheek. But sleep continued to elude her. She switched on the light impatiently to reach for the paperback copy of Hardy's *Wessex Tales* that lay on the bedside table. At last she slept.

She was on the point of leaving the house the next

morning when the telephone rang. She answered it, thinking that perhaps it was Miriam to say that she couldn't come into work for some reason. Instead it was Garel, the phone italicising the charismatic timbre of his voice.

'Hello, Elin.'

'Garel!' she exclaimed with a little laugh of pleasure. She hadn't expected him to ring, since he'd phoned the previous evening. 'If you'd called a minute later I'd have already left for the boutique.'

'Then I'm glad I caught you. I wanted to hear your voice,' he said. 'The night was so lonely without you.'

'For me, too,' she admitted. 'I read until late.'

'A book's a poor bed-mate.'

The sensual note in his tone quickened her pulse. Her voice a shade husky, she asked, 'Is the conference going well? What time will you be home on Friday?'

'Around seven, I should think. I won't stay on the line any longer or I'll make you late for work. I'll see you on Friday, *cariad*.'

Feeling happy, she put the receiver down. They would soon be together again. Although she was busy at work, her thoughts returned frequently to sharing a family with him. He had said he wanted children. It would give her such pleasure, she realised, to tell him she was pregnant.

She found she was impatient for his homecoming as, on Friday evening, she surveyed the dining-room table. The silver gleamed against the embroidered linen cloth she had bought on their honeymoon in Tenerife.

She moved the flower arrangement an inch, so that the gypsophila didn't brush the bottle of red wine. She had deliberately chosen the same flowers for the centrepiece that had been in her wedding bouquet. The candles, tall and slim in their silver holders, added another romantic note to the table.

In the kitchen a moussaka was cooking in the oven. There was a lemon sorbet in the refrigerator, together with the melon she planned to serve as a starter. Everything was ready for Garel's arrival, including herself.

She had changed into a beguilingly feminine dress that was patterned in swirls of dusky pink and white with a mandarin collar, neat waist and a cut-away back that revealed a triangle of bare skin, the apex of the cut-away at the nape of her neck. Its full skirt fell to an inch or two above her ankles, flattering each graceful movement she made. With it she wore high heeled sandals, while the fragrance that surrounded her was Estée Lauder's 'Beautiful'.

A car drew to a halt in front of the house. Quick to hear it, she was already in the hall when the doorbell rang. She opened the front door wide, her smile of welcome promptly fading as, instead of her husband, she saw Felicity.

In a linen suit, with a beautifully cut jacket and her coppery hair caught back in a black bow, his PA looked smart and efficient. Tucked under her arm was a beige folder.

'Is Garel home?' she began airily.

'No, not yet,' Elin answered.

'I've got some papers he said he wanted to look over at the weekend.'

'I'll see that he gets them,' Elin told her.

'I'm not in a rush. I don't mind waiting, and I'd rather give them to him personally,' Felicity answered.

With little option to do otherwise, Elin invited her

in. Sam, who had been curled up in one of the armchairs in the lounge, lifted his head at the sound of their voices. As Felicity entered the room he jumped down on to the carpet, slid his body low under the chair and, the moment Felicity's back was to him, stalked silently out of the door.

Elin doubted that Felicity had even noticed him. With a touch of wry amusement, it occurred to her that her cat took to her husband's PA little better than she did.

'I see you've made some changes in the lounge,' Felicity announced, setting the folder down on the coffee-table and glancing about her as she sat on the sofa.

'A few,' Elin agreed.

'I suppose you wanted to put your mark on the house.' There was a faintly derisive note in Felicity's voice.

'Garel likes a few feminine touches to make it homely,' Elin answered, her tone coolly polite.

Getting up from her seat, Felicity strolled over to the fireplace to look at the autumn landscape that was hung on the chimney breast. Idly she remarked, 'I see that, despite the alterations, one of Carol's pictures still has pride of place.'

'Carol's?' Elin echoed, her startled gaze swinging to the picture.

A gleam of satisfaction came into the violet eyes that studied her. 'Didn't you know Garel's wife was an artist?' Felicity asked silkily.

Since her row with Garel, Elin had forgotten her uneasiness about his feelings for his dead wife. Now with Felicity's words it suddenly came back. But, determined not to reveal her jealousy of Carol to

Felicity, she answered with a negligent shrug, 'Garel rarely talks about Carol. He doesn't live in the past.'

'You think not?' Felicity retorted maliciously. A baiting smile about her lips, she went on, 'Ironic, isn't it, that neither of us really got him?'

'I'm afraid I don't know what you mean.'

'Isn't it obvious?' Felicity asked derisively. 'Garel's the sort of man to love only once.' She paused before delivering the shot, 'And he loved Carol, his first wife.'

Elin's mouth tightened. Her nails were beginning to make marks in her palms, but, covering the vague uncertainty she felt about Garel's love for her, she answered coolly, 'If that were true he wouldn't have remarried.'

Hard spite glinted in Felicity's violet eyes as she said, 'All he wanted was a suitable corporate wife, someone to help him entertain, someone who'd be the rose in his buttonhole on social occasions. Don't be under any illusions. If I'd had your background, he'd have married me.'

Elin got to her feet. It was only the fact that Felicity was a visitor to her house that helped her to exhibit such control. Her voice chill, she said, 'Well, he didn't. And, furthermore, my husband isn't in love with a ghost.'

'Isn't he?' Felicity snapped, before immediately furnishing the answer. 'When Garel realises you can't fill Carol's place, you'll lose him.'

'I suggest, Felicity, you find a husband of your own instead of coveting mine!'

Her remark brought the slim redhead surging to her feet.

'Garel would have *been* my husband if you hadn't

shown up,' she said venomously.

The sound of a key turning in the front door made Elin check her reply. A moment later Garel strode into the lounge, tall and arrestingly attractive in a charcoal-grey business suit and white shirt.

Jolted as she was by Felicity's stinging comments, Elin was determined not to let them alter the way she'd planned to greet her husband. Immediately she went towards him, sliding her arms around his neck as she stood on tiptoe to kiss him. Drawing back, she smiled, her heartbeat quickened from her fleeting contact with his firm lips.

'It's lovely to have you home.'

'It's nice to get such a warm welcome,' he replied. Keeping his arm around her waist, he greeted his PA. 'Hello, Fliss. I noticed your car as I turned into the drive. I wasn't expecting to see you till Monday.'

'I thought you'd want to look at the spread sheets on budgeted sales for the Manakos group, so I brought them round.'

'That was good of you,' Garel said.

He moved to take the folder from her which she had picked up from the coffee-table. Stabbing Elin a quick inimical look, Felicity stood by his shoulder as he opened it. A polished fingernail drew his attention to the figures on the top sheet.

'You can see the group will be in overdraft for the whole of the autumn quarter,' she said.

Garel nodded thoughtfully and, feeling somewhat *de trop*, Elin stated, 'I must check on things in the kitchen. Dinner's almost ready.'

Glancing up, he answered, 'Fine.'

In the kitchen she turned down the oven before leaning against the worktop. She bit her lip, her expressive green eyes a mirror of her distress. However competent Felicity was as a PA, as a woman she was poisonous. Elin didn't want to believe a word she had said. She wouldn't have done, had she not realised that never once had Garel actually said he loved her.

Angrily she told herself to stop it. She had accepted when she had agreed to marry him that she might always have to take second place in his heart to Carol. But that didn't mean she wasn't important to him.

She thought of the dark intensity in his eyes when they made love, the smouldering passion with which he reached for her, the tender zeal of his mouth as it claimed hers, his protectiveness towards her. Of course he loved her. Maybe not as he had loved his first wife, but perhaps in time, perhaps when they shared a family together . . .

'Dinner smells good.'

Garel's voice made her start. Quickly she roused herself as he advanced into the kitchen, realising that Felicity must have gone.

'I've made an aubergine moussaka,' she said. 'I know it's a favourite of yours.'

'Moussaka, a bottle of Barbaresco to go with it, candles on the dining-room table,' he teased. 'It appears that absence really does make the heart grow fonder.' He took hold of her hands and pulled her against him, tilting up her chin to ask, 'Does this mean we'll be having an early night?'

Despair went through her at his words, despair mingled with anger. She enjoyed going to bed with him, but for her sex was a means of expressing her love. His comments made her feel that for him it was nothing more than an act of pleasurable possession.

Her eyes stormy, she snapped, 'Sometimes I think the only relationship we have is a physical one.'

Her flash of temper seemed to amuse him.

'Don't knock it, my love,' he said. 'You're a great joy to me in bed.'

His arms were hard around her, and she tried to push them away. But it was a waste of effort, for the next instant he bent his head, holding her in a grip that was prepared to tolerate no resistance as he sought her mouth.

His shoulders seemed to dwarf her with their breadth. She felt her breasts crushed against the warm plane of his chest. His kiss was plundering and intimate, sending a lick of fire along her veins, and before it ended she had her arms around his neck and was kissing him back with equal passion.

When his dark head lifted, her lashes fluttered up. There was a glint of tigerish satisfaction in his eyes as he studied her faintly flushed face. Caressing the softness of her cheek with the back of his fingers, he said throatily, 'I've missed you, Elin.'

The throb in his deep voice sent a shiver tingling down her spine. 'I've missed you, too,' she admitted in a husky whisper. 'Terribly.'

He smiled before bending to her lips again. In his arms she forgot they were in the kitchen, failed to notice that the clock had ticked on past the twenty minutes needed to brown the moussaka. It was only when he lifted his mouth from hers that she realised that the meal was more than ready.

When at last they were seated opposite each other in the dining-room, the candles flickering in the slight breeze from the open window, it didn't seem to matter that the main course she had gone to so much trouble with was a little burned on top. As they ate Garel told her about the conference he had just attended, making her laugh with his anecdotes.

Later she led the way into the lounge. She poured the coffee and then kicked off her shoes as she sat down on the sofa beside him. He reached out and pulled her to him, not to kiss her, but to run his hand caressingly down her arm as she leaned her head against his shoulder.

'By the way,' he murmured, 'I've got tickets for *South Pacific*. You mentioned the other day you'd like to see it.'

'But you don't like musicals,' she said, a trace of puzzled laughter in her voice.

'Not as much as you do, perhaps,' he conceded. 'But I think anyone would enjoy *South Pacific*. It's got some good tunes.'

She smiled, certain he had got the tickets just to please her.

'When are we going?' she asked.

'Next Wednesday,' he told her. 'I thought that would suit you as you close early that day. Do you want to meet me at the theatre, or at my office?'

'I'll meet you at the theatre.' There was a short easy silence between them, and then she said, 'Did I tell you that Dad phoned last night?'

'How is he?'

'He's fine. He says he's looking forward to visiting us at the end of September.' She disengaged herself from his embrace to set her coffee-cup aside, and added, 'He teased me a bit about not wanting to wait too long for grandchildren at his age.'

Sitting forward on the sofa, she missed the speculative look Garel gave her.

'I didn't think you'd want to give up the boutique for a while yet,' he commented.

'I wouldn't have to,' she answered. 'Miriam could run it for most of the time if I took on another assistant, and things like ordering stock I could do from home. If necessary we could even have paid help in the house for a while.'

He didn't answer immediately and, not understanding the cause of his silence, she turned her head swiftly to glance at him to know what he was thinking. The dark intimacy of his eyes as they met hers created havoc with her senses.

'You seem to have given it some thought,' he said, a questioning note in his sensual voice.

The air seemed suddenly charged with the electric awareness between them. His nearness made the impact of his virility all the more powerful, the magnetism of attraction that linked them starting a pulse-beat thumping in her throat. Huskily she admitted, 'While you've been away, I have.'

He drew a long, almost shuddering breath, taking her hand in his and bending to put his lips to her palm. Her lashes fluttered as she trembled and he looked up, his eyes holding hers, a leaping fire in their dark depths.

'You bewitch me, Elin,' he muttered thickly, pulling her on to his lap to kiss her in a searching, almost starving way.

The hunger of his mouth sparked off a response in her that made it seem as if all the recent nights without him were accumulated into a need as fierce as his own. Winding her arms tightly around his neck, she kissed him back with an ardour that inflamed him.

He stood up, lifting her high against his chest to

carry her upstairs to their bed, his weight as he
followed her down on to the mattress sending a
shudder of mindless rapture through her. In minutes
he had dispensed with her clothing, his branding kisses
searing her skin. Feverish and gasping with the force
of her desire, she pushed his shirt from his shoulders,
slipping the buckle of his belt free.

The mutual need was so intense that there was no
time for leisurely lovemaking. Instead there was an
almost frantic urgency to their union. She cried out,
her fingers digging into his shoulders as the vortex
claimed her, her body so perfectly in tune with his that
the blinding moment of release came at the same time
as his groaning shudder of consummation.

When the raging tide of passion receded she lay
spent and dazed by the pleasure he had given her, the
ripples of response echoing through her body. Still
breathing hard, Garel moved a little to cradle her
against his chest. She pressed her lips to his throat
before slipping almost instantly into a chasm of sleep,
the serenity in her face testifying to the complete
catharsis of their lovemaking.

It was morning before she stirred. Stretching
languorously, she opened her eyes to discover he was
already up. She watched him for a moment, caught by
the sheer animal grace of him. In jeans, with his bare
chest gleaming bronze in the sunlight, and with his
dark hair ruffled, he was arrestingly male, virility
stamped into every line and plane of him. Her heart
contracted with the love she felt for him.

It was as he reached out for his shirt that she saw
the scratches on his back, long red marks left by her
nails, which bore witness to the primitive hunger of
their lovemaking. In retrospect her fierce

overwhelming need of him shocked her. Her breath
caught in her throat and, as it did so, Garel turned his
head. He smiled faintly as he saw the direction of her
gaze.

'Did I do that last night?' she said in a whisper,
lifting her gaze to his face.

'I'm flattered,' he answered. She coloured, and he
came and sat down on the bed to ask in a lazy,
caressing voice that had a hint of amusement in it,
'What's the matter? You're behaving as though you've
something to be ashamed of.'

'It's just that we've never made love quite like that
before,' she murmured, embarrassment deepening her
blush.

He leaned over and trailed his lips across her bare
shoulder.

'You're a very passionate woman,' he said against
her skin, his deep, husky voice quickening her senses.

He lifted his head, the line of his lips resolute as
ever, but his eyes smiled at her and her own answered
them. He kissed her mouth lingeringly before getting
up off the bed. She reached for her wrap and drew it
on. It was crazy to be shy with him after all the intimate
moments they had shared, but the dark light in his eyes
made her tantalisingly aware of her nakedness.

Studying her, Garel asked, 'Did you mean what you
said yesterday evening about wanting a baby so soon?'

His question took her unawares, and she answered,
'Yes. Why? I thought you wanted a family too.'

'I do,' he confirmed. 'I was just curious as to why
you and Roger didn't start a family.'

'He wasn't very keen on the idea,' she told him, 'and
the marriage never seemed stable enough to bring
children into it.'

'But you think our marriage is,' Garel said.

It wasn't a question, yet, because Felicity's words still lingered somewhere in the recesses of her mind, she questioned anxiously, 'Don't you?'

Pulling her into his arms, he growled deep in his throat.

'I never intend letting you go. Surely you know that by now?'

# CHAPTER TEN

THE train as far as Baker Street was almost empty. It was once Elin had changed on to the Circle Line that she was caught up in the commuter crush. The Piccadilly Line was even more crowded. Squeezed in tightly against the doors of a train that was crammed with fellow passengers, Elin found it suffocatingly hot and airless.

She had planned to go straight to Leicester Square, but, freeing her cramped arm to glance at her wrist-watch, she changed her mind. The journey hadn't taken her as long as she had expected. Rather than stay on the packed train and then have to kill time while she waited for Garel at the theatre, she decide to get out at Holborn to join him at his office.

The long clanking escalators carried her up to street-level where she handed in her ticket. Glad to be out in the fresh air and among the noise of the traffic, she walked briskly.

Her husband's company occupied a suite of offices on the fourth floor of a tower block with an impressive frontage. She pushed open the swing doors and went inside, her court shoes tapping as she crossed the elegant marble-floored foyer. The building was quiet at this time of the evening.

She identified herself to the security officer on the desk and then went up to the fourth floor in the lift. It opened on to a spacious reception area. The thick carpeting muffled the sound of her footsteps as she walked along the corridor and into the outer office which connected with Garel's. As she had expected it was empty, and the cover was on the typewriter on the desk. Felicity had obviously gone home.

She would have walked straight into the inner office to surprise Garel, had not the murmur of voices from behind the door, with its opaque glass window, told her he had someone with him. She couldn't hear what he was saying, but the timbre of his deep voice was audible, making a slight furrow appear between her brows. Whatever he was discussing, it plainly wasn't business.

The next moment a woman's shadow was framed behind the glass. She heard Felicity say something in a slightly raised but indistinct voice. Her lips compressed, and she was on the point of interrupting when her husband's tall dark shadow also appeared. He took Felicity into his arms, the two blurred silhouettes joining as one.

Emotion drained the colour from Elin's face. With her gaze still fixed on the dim but eloquent picture behind the glass, she reversed one step at a time towards the open door behind her, before suddenly her numbed disbelief yielded to an agony of pain. With a strangled sob she ran from the outer office, banging her shoulder against the door-jamb in her haste to escape.

She pressed the button for the lift and then, when the doors didn't open immediately, she went to the stairs. She fled down them as though she could somehow outrun the emotion that was tearing her apart. In minutes she was out in the street.

A driver blew at her as she stepped blindly off the kerb, his car screeching to a halt only a couple of feet

away from her. Too upset to realise she could have
been knocked down, she obeyed the angry wave of the
man's hand and crossed in front of the bonnet of his
car.

It had never entered her mind that her husband
would be unfaithful to her. Felicity's voice echoed
mockingly in her memory. 'When Garel realises you
can't take Carol's place, you'll lose him.'

Yet in what way had she failed him? she asked
herself in angry despair. Certainly not in bed. Just to
think of their lovemaking was to feel another
knife-thrust of betrayal. A tear ran down her cheek,
and she brushed it away as she walked on, not wanting
to cry in the street and to have people stare at her.

She had refused to believe that Garel had only
married her because he wanted a suitable wife from a
suitable background. But evidently it was the truth.
From his point of view the sexual rapport they shared
was simply a bonus.

A strangling tightness gripped her throat. She had
to stop thinking about what Felicity had said. She'd go
crazy with the pain if she didn't. Somehow she must
cling to the myth that Garel had married her because
he loved her.

She found herself on the Embankment and turned
in the direction of Westminster Bridge, the beauty of
the Thames making no impact on her at all. Why had
Garel had to reappear in her life? she wondered, her
eyes stinging. She had been happy enough in her
independence before she had met him again. She
hadn't wanted to love or trust again. It had hurt too
much the first time.

Her sharply indrawn breath was almost a sob. She
pressed her lips together more tightly. She would not

cry. She would not! Keep it in perspective, she told herself fiercely. It was only a kiss. Maybe there had been a reason for it. Maybe it wasn't quite the way it had looked.

For a moment the charm worked, and then, with sudden fury, she cast it aside. Was she going to find excuses for Garel's lapses in fidelity in the same way that while she had been married to Roger she had tried to excuse his sudden outbursts of violent temper?

She was scarcely aware of the route she took, of skirting St James's Park and then, some time later, of passing beneath Admiralty Arch. The light was fading, but it wasn't till she reached the Aldwych that she realised where she was. She had wanted to put as much distance between her and Garel as possible. Yet ironically her footsteps had brought her back to within a stone's throw of his office.

The thought made her suddenly remember that she was supposed to be at the theatre. Instead of being at his office, Garel would now be standing in the foyer wondering where on earth she was. She wasn't ready yet to face him, but with no other alternative she hailed a taxi.

She sat back in the cab, her anguish hardening into a tight-clenched knot of anger. She had already decided she wasn't going to confront him with what she had seen. Her love for him was the core of her life. She stood to lose too much if she demanded frankness from him about his relationship with Felicity. If he refused to give her up, Elin's life would crumble to pieces. And, whatever she was going through now, it was preferable to the hell of losing him altogether.

The taxi dropped her right outside the theatre. She paid the driver and, with an act that was as good as any that was going on stage, she went unconcernedly up the wide steps and into the foyer.

Garel was pacing across the expanse of deep maroon carpet. His black hair gleamed in the lights from the chandeliers, his expensive dark suit emphasising his masculine aura of power and success. She thought she had her emotions reasonably in check but, seeing him, a rage of hurt welled up inside her again.

His gaze swung to her and she took in the hard-set look on his chiselled face. He was angry with her for being late, and she was glad of it. The desire to strike back at him, if only a little, made her begin with a feigned innocence she knew would annoy him still further.

'I'm sorry. Have I kept you waiting?'

'Where the hell have you been?' he demanded. 'I've been worried about you. You're more than an hour late.'

'Am I really?' she said as though surprised. She shrugged. 'I must have forgotten the time. You know how it is.'

'No,' he said grittily. 'I *don't* know how it is.'

'How long is it till the interval when we can take our seats?' she asked, cutting across him in the same tone of light unconcern.

His hand clamped down on her arm. 'I phoned the boutique and I phoned you at home. There was no reply from either place. Now where the hell have you been?'

'Checking up on me?' she snapped sarcastically.

'You said you wanted to see this show,' he reminded her, curbed anger in his voice. 'It was hard to get tickets, but, having gone to the trouble of getting them,

I didn't expect you to breeze up over an hour late with the excuse that you forgot the time.'

'It's very easy to get wrapped up in things. I'm sure you find that too.'

'Just what exactly am I supposed to infer from that remark?' he fired back.

'You can infer from it anything you like! Now let go of my arm. I've missed enough of the show as it is. I don't want to miss any more.'

'We can miss the whole damn lot as far as I'm concerned,' he said gratingly.

'Since you didn't want to see the show in the first place, that, of course, would be your attitude!' she retorted.

His mouth thinned. She knew she'd pressed her luck with that last comment even before he marshalled her across the foyer towards the swing doors as though she were some prisoner under guard. He waited until they were outside on the pavement before saying with quiet ferocity, 'I don't know what the devil's got into you, but we're going to thrash this out.'

She glared back into Garel's glittering dark eyes. 'Finding me troublesome?' she jeered, her voice shaking a little with the intensity of all the pain and fury she was holding back. 'What a shame. Especially when what you wanted was a wife who'd be no trouble, someone who'd play the part of hostess to impress your business associates and who'd provide you with a suitable heir!'

She saw his jaw clench. 'I warn you, Elin,' he said quietly. 'You have gone far enough for one evening.'

His dangerously calm tone advised her to hold her tongue. She clenched her teeth on the answer she might otherwise have made. As he propelled her along the street, his grip clamped on her arm, she demanded with muted antagonism, 'Where are we going?'

'Where do you think?' he fired back. 'Home's the only place for the sort of discussion you and I are going to have.'

Not daring to defy him by stating that she had no intention of discussing anything with him, she said pettishly, 'I hope the car's parked somewhere near. My feet ache and I can't walk much further.'

His hawkish brows came together as he slanted a sharp glance of enquiry at her. Curtly he answered, 'It's a little strange to be complaining about walking a short distance to the car when you've come all the way on the tube. Where exactly have you been on foot this evening?'

Angered by what she had accidentally let slip, and by his quick perceptiveness, she flashed, 'Are you setting yourself up as a detective? Because I've done some snooping of my own!'

His grip tightened ominously on her arm, but in a voice that was almost pleasant he said, 'You can tell me what you mean by that, either in the car, or when we get home, whichever you prefer.'

She didn't answer. She knew she couldn't trust her voice.

In the car she sat beside him in wretched silence while the power-hungry Jaguar sped along the streets. She hated the way she was behaving that was so totally out of character, the barbed things she had said.

A tear spilled down her cheek and, not wanting him to see it, she averted her head. Resting her elbow on the sill of the passenger window, she pressed her knuckles tightly against her trembling lips and stared out. A sense of bitter futility enveloped her. What chance was there for their marriage when Garel didn't love her and when, now that she'd seen him kissing Felicity, she couldn't stop playing the shrew? Another tear splashed on to her knuckles.

She thought she heard Garel swear under his breath. Pride made her jerk her head up as he demanded tersely, 'Are you crying?'

'No, of course not,' she denied in a muffled voice.

When he brought the car to a halt outside their house she was slow in making a move. She was still unfastening her seatbelt when Garel opened her door for her from the outside. She forgot to pick up her bag that was lying on the dashboard, and obligingly he reached into the Jaguar to hand it to her.

He unlocked the front door and stood back for her to enter the house ahead of him. She did so, darting a wary glance at his face, noting the tightness of his jaw and the hard light in his eyes.

She knew all the warning signs. For all his customary chivalrous behaviour towards her, there was no relaxation in him, only a methodical preparation for the attack. What alarmed her was that, despite her resolve not to give rein to her temper, there was an answering tension and anger inside herself, every bit as fierce, just waiting to be released.

She set her bag down on the hall table and said with false composure, 'I don't know about you, but I'd love a cup of tea.'

'We've plenty of time,' he agreed calmly. 'Why not?'

She knew exactly what he meant by that comment, but she didn't rise to it. Instead she went into the kitchen, filled the electric kettle and plugged it in. Garel stood in the doorway, watching her.

She rattled two cups into their saucers, her nerves tightening in the unnatural silence. The skin at the back of her neck began to prickle. Even the poised vigilance of his body seemed somehow a threat. Finally she couldn't endure the tense atmosphere and his unnerving stare any longer.

Abruptly she switched off the singing kettle and said tightly, 'I've changed my mind about wanting a drink.'

Garel stepped aside as she approached him, allowing her to sweep past him into the hall. His forbearance surprised her, because he wasn't the sort of man to stand for much nonsense from anyone.

But her sense of relief came too soon. She had her hand on the newel when his ominously calm voice made her start.

'Just where do you think you're going?'

'I'm going to bed.'

'That's where you're wrong.'

Her heart was thumping unevenly, but she managed to say firmly, 'I can't see any point in——'

She broke off with a gasp as Garel snatched hold of her by the arm and pushed her ahead of him into the lounge.

In the centre of the room he released her. He stood between her and the door, a dark, ferocious man whose patience she had finally exhausted.

'You don't seem to have paid much attention to what I said to you earlier,' he remarked, the quietness of his voice italicising its ruthlessness. 'I said I wanted an explanation from you.'

She had never heard him use quite that tone of voice with her before. She clenched her hands that had begun to tremble. Swallowing, she said stiffly, trying hard to match her tone to the words of her apology, 'I'm sorry about what happened this evening. I'll try to be more punctual in future. Now can we just forget it?

'No, Elin. Not this time.'

'What do you mean, not this time?'

'You've acted in this unreasonable way with me once before—five years ago, to be precise.'

He took a step towards her and she willed herself to hold her ground.

'Don't think you can back me into a corner,' she flared, 'because you can't.'

'Sit down!'

'No!' she refused defiantly, and then gave a tiny cry of protest as he pushed her into an armchair.

She made to scramble to her feet, but he shoved her back, leaning over her, his eyes glittering dangerously. Her mouth dry, she shrank away as he said, 'You've had as much leeway as I'm prepared to give you. You're going to tell me what it is that's eating you.'

She glared at him, her fear suddenly forgotten as he reminded her of the cause of her anger.

'*Nothing* is eating me!' she snapped.

'You'd better start explaining, Elin,' he warned, 'because I'm not inclined to be tolerant with you any longer.'

'Don't try to bully me! I'm only sorry I was ever fool enough to marry you!'

A nerve jumped in his jaw. With the relentless purpose of a trained interrogator, he said, 'Where were you this evening?'

'I don't expect you to play the heavy-handed husband because I was a few minutes late showing up at the theatre,' she answered.

Her voice caught a little and he straightened slowly. Ready to hold her down if she made any move to escape, he said in an even tone, 'We'll try again. Where were you?'

'I was walking along by the Embankment,' she capitulated resentfully. 'There, does that satisfy you?'

'Not entirely,' he snapped. 'But at least we're finally getting somewhere. What were you doing on the Embankment?'

'Why?' she flashed. 'What are you accusing me of? Having an assignation with someone? After all, James works near there.'

'Let me make it clear,' he said grimly. 'You may have your regrets about having married me, but if you so much as even give me cause to suspect you of sleeping with another man you'll more than rue the day I put my ring on your finger.'

'You mean it's all right for *you* to have the odd fling, but *I've* got to be faithful——' She broke off, only to burst out suddenly with all the vehemence of pain, 'I wish I'd married James. I wish I'd married anyone but you!'

'Then why didn't you marry James?' Garel demanded. 'He was besotted enough with you to have asked you if you'd given him the least encouragement.'

'Because I *trusted* you!' she cried. She got to her feet, her eyes blazing as she rushed on bitterly, 'Well, at last I've learned to expect nothing from men—not honesty, not fidelity, not even love!'

'You think that statement surprises me?' Garel said savagely, grabbing hold of her by the shoulders. 'That bastard of a first husband of yours really did a good job on you, didn't he? He left you more than just physically scarred. Five years ago you were a warm, spontaneous woman. Now you're so distrustful I'd find it pitiful to watch if it didn't make me so angry.

'I thought I could make you forget everything he put you through, but I was wrong. Right now you're hurting. I know you are, and I want you to tell me why so that maybe I can put it right. But you're so walled up behind those defences of yours, I just can't get through to you, can I?'

'Yes, you have hurt me,' she stormed. 'But don't think you ever will again. From now on I'm going to be as hard and untouchable as that glass bowl you gave me.'

Releasing her, Garel crossed the room with angry strides. He picked up the object she had mentioned, and in a single gesture he hurled it at the stone fireplace. The glass bowl shattered in a myriad glittering, tinkling pieces.

He swung back to her furiously, his expression changing as he saw the look of horror on her face. She was shaking violently, her eyes wide with fear. He came towards her in immediate concern as sobs began to rack her.

'Oh, God!' he muttered in a tormented voice. 'Elin, I'm sorry.'

He gathered her into his strong, comforting arms. The moment of pure instinctive dread had passed even before she heard him speak. With her fingers closing on a fistful of his shirt, she gave way to a storm of tears.

'Don't cry,' Garel murmured in a low, ragged voice. 'Please, sweetheart, don't cry. I didn't think . . . Darling, don't. I forgot for a minute how easily you get scared.'

She wanted to tell him she wasn't afraid now, to explain that it was a reflex reaction which had made her blanch when he had broken the bowl, but she was shaking and crying so hard that she couldn't get the words out.

He held her close, his hand resting against the back of her head. In the haven of his embrace she wept until she ran dry of tears. Garel ran his palm soothingly over her dark hair. Pressing his lips against her temple, he whispered, 'I'm going to clear up this glass and then we're going to talk.' He tilted her chin up and she gave a little convulsive catch of breath. Looking down into her swimming eyes, he said gently, 'You don't have to cry any more, *cariad*. There'll be no more shouting tonight.'

She stayed on the sofa as he had ordered her to do while he dealt with the broken glass. She felt very tired, too drained of emotion to do anything but sit passively. It was as she watched him sweep up the last fragments, the chiselled planes of his face accentuated by the shadows in the room, that her throat began to ache.

In a cramped whisper, she said, 'I came to your office this evening. That's why I was late meeting you at the theatre.'

His gaze swung to her. Leaving what he was doing, he got to his feet.

'If you were at my office, why didn't you come in?'

Clasping her hands tightly together, she said in a pinched voice, 'Because . . . because I saw you kissing Felicity.'

'You what?' he exploded with angry disbelief. He paused, as though to curb his temper, and then demanded with harsh exasperation, 'What sort of man do you think I am?'

'I saw your shadows behind the glass,' she whispered wretchedly.

'And that's all you did see,' he fired back, 'a play of shadows, because, however it might have looked, I wasn't kissing Felicity.'

Her stricken green eyes lifted to his face, a spark of hope kindling in them. His jawline was tight, but he kept his forceful voice even as he said, 'The other day Fliss went for a job interview with another firm. She very much hoped to get it because it involves a lot of travelling abroad with all expenses paid. Well, today the company phoned to offer her the job, and this evening we were talking about it.

'I don't know at what point in our conversation you must have come into the outer office, but I was offering her my congratulations once again, and telling her how sorry I'd be to lose her, when she said tearfully that she was going to hate leaving. I gave her my handkerchief and put an arm round her. I think she put her head on my shoulder for a few minutes. And that, my suspicious little wife, is all that happened.'

Elin struggled to find her voice. The emotional release made her want to start crying again. She knew she had angered him with her mistrust, and, trying to put things right, to offer some warrant for her suspicions, she said huskily, 'Felicity told me you'd only married me because you wanted a suitable corporate wife, that you were still in love with Carol.'

'When?' he demanded. 'This evening at the office? She couldn't have. We left the building together.'

'No, the other day when she called round at the house.'

Garel drew a deep breath and then said quietly,

'Well, I suppose that explains everything I wanted to know.'

He started to move away from the fireplace. Thinking he intended leaving the room, Elin sprang to her feet, knowing she had to stop him. In a choked voice, she pleaded, 'Garel, please don't turn away from me. I'm sorry I mistrusted you, but, please . . . I'll make it up to you. I . . . I love you and . . .'

A sob snatched the end of her sentence again. The tears came once more before she could check them. With a smothered exclamation he was across the room to her, pulling her into his arms.

Tilting up her chin, he said with rough tenderness, 'You're still running scared, aren't you? You still haven't realised how very much I love you.'

Her lips parted. With those three magical words he had rescued her from a nightmare of uncertainty. It was like being snatched out of a dark pit and the brightness was almost dazzling. As his embrace tightened she wound her arms urgently around his neck, happiness coursing through her, happiness and an intense, trembling, overwhelming relief.

'I thought . . .' she whispered. 'I thought you were comparing me with Carol all the time.'

'I've never once compared you!' he said, as though thunderstruck. Easing her away from him so he could look down at her, he went on, 'Listen to me, *cariad*, Carol and I were childhood sweethearts. What I felt for her was an abiding companionable love. But what I feel for you is no less deep, and no less precious.'

She looked up at him, all that was in her heart mirrored in the hot glow of her eyes. With a groan he combed his fingers into her hair, bending to her lips almost as a man parched by the sun might seek water.

Arched tightly to him, she kissed him back, her heart racing with everything that his deeply passionate kiss promised.

When at last he raised his head it was to smile down at her and to say huskily, 'I'll never forget the day I met you. You were working in the design-room of your father's mill with the sunlight gleaming on your hair, and suddenly from across the room you looked at me with those emerald-green eyes of yours. It was like some thunderbolt.'

'You made quite an impression on me too,' she whispered, a thread of laughter in her voice.

'When you told me our night together meant nothing to you, I was furious. I swore I'd put you out of my mind, and then I was more furious still because I couldn't. Losing you to Roger was bad enough, but if I'd known how he was treating you I think I'd have almost killed him.'

A muscle twitched in his jaw and she reached up a slim hand, her fingers trailing a caress along his swarthy skin.

'That was why you were so angry when I told you Roger had a violent temper,' she murmured.

He caught her hand in his, opening it to press a kiss into her palm.

'Even now the thought of him striking you enrages me,' he growled.

'It's all over now,' she whispered. 'It's in the past. You've made me feel safe again.'

'Have I?' he asked. 'You're still afraid to have a good row with me. If I hadn't really pushed you tonight you'd have bottled up everything you were feeling rather than confront me with it.'

'I know, but not any more,' she said. 'I've learned

now that I don't have to be afraid of my temper or of yours.'

Tender amusement tempered the glitter of passion in his eyes.

'You've quite a fiery temper when you let yourself go,' he teased.

'What would you expect from a Celt?' she joked.

She gave a gasp of laughter as he swept her off her feet and answered, 'A passionate nature to go with it.'

And then her laughter was lost in a dizzying excitement as he sought her mouth again. She realised he was carrying her upstairs, and tightened her arms round his neck. With no barriers left between them, theirs was to be a night of wild, sweet love.

# "INDULGE A LITTLE" SWEEPSTAKES

## HERE'S HOW THE SWEEPSTAKES WORKS

### NO PURCHASE NECESSARY

To enter each drawing, complete the appropriate Official Entry Form or a 3" by 5" index card by hand-printing your name, address and phone number and the trip destination that the entry is being submitted for (i.e., Walt Disney World Vacation Drawing, etc.) and mailing it to: Indulge '91 Subscribers-Only Sweepstakes, P.O. Box 1397, Buffalo, New York 14269-1397.

No responsibility is assumed for lost, late or misdirected mail. Entries must be sent separately with first class postage affixed, and be received by: 9/30/91 for the Walt Disney World Vacation Drawing, 10/31/91 for the Alaskan Cruise Drawing and 11/30/91 for the Hawaiian Vacation Drawing. Sweepstakes is open to residents of the U.S. and Canada, 21 years of age or older as of 11/7/91.

For complete rules, send a self-addressed, stamped (WA residents need not affix return postage) envelope to: Indulge '91 Subscribers-Only Sweepstakes Rules, P.O. Box 4005, Blair, NE 68009.

© 1991 HARLEQUIN ENTERPRISES LTD.                                              DIR-RL

---

# "INDULGE A LITTLE" SWEEPSTAKES

## HERE'S HOW THE SWEEPSTAKES WORKS

### NO PURCHASE NECESSARY

To enter each drawing, complete the appropriate Official Entry Form or a 3" by 5" index card by hand-printing your name, address and phone number and the trip destination that the entry is being submitted for (i.e., Walt Disney World Vacation Drawing, etc.) and mailing it to: Indulge '91 Subscribers-Only Sweepstakes, P.O. Box 1397, Buffalo, New York 14269-1397.

No responsibility is assumed for lost, late or misdirected mail. Entries must be sent separately with first class postage affixed, and be received by: 9/30/91 for the Walt Disney World Vacation Drawing, 10/31/91 for the Alaskan Cruise Drawing and 11/30/91 for the Hawaiian Vacation Drawing. Sweepstakes is open to residents of the U.S. and Canada, 21 years of age or older as of 11/7/91.

For complete rules, send a self-addressed, stamped (WA residents need not affix return postage) envelope to: Indulge '91 Subscribers-Only Sweepstakes Rules, P.O. Box 4005, Blair, NE 68009.

© 1991 HARLEQUIN ENTERPRISES LTD.                                              DIR-RL

## INDULGE A LITTLE—WIN A LOT!

## Summer of '91 Subscribers-Only Sweepstakes

# OFFICIAL ENTRY FORM

This entry must be received by: Sept. 30, 1991
This month's winner will be notified by: Oct. 7, 1991
Trip must be taken between: Nov. 7, 1991—Nov. 7, 1992

**YES,** I want to win the Walt Disney World® vacation for two. I understand the prize includes round-trip airfare, first-class hotel and pocket money as revealed on the "wallet" scratch-off card.

Name _____

Address_____ Apt. _____

City _____

State/Prov. _____ Zip/Postal Code _____

Daytime phone number _____
(Area Code)

Return entries with invoice in envelope provided. Each book in this shipment has two entry coupons—and the more coupons you enter, the better your chances of winning!

© 1991 HARLEQUIN ENTERPRISES LTD.                    CPS-M1

---

## INDULGE A LITTLE—WIN A LOT!

## Summer of '91 Subscribers-Only Sweepstakes

# OFFICIAL ENTRY FORM

This entry must be received by: Sept. 30, 1991
This month's winner will be notified by: Oct. 7, 1991
Trip must be taken between: Nov. 7, 1991—Nov. 7, 1992

**YES,** I want to win the Walt Disney World® vacation for two. I understand the prize includes round-trip airfare, first-class hotel and pocket money as revealed on the "wallet" scratch-off card.

Name _____

Address_____ Apt. _____

City _____

State/Prov. _____ Zip/Postal Code _____

Daytime phone number _____
(Area Code)

Return entries with invoice in envelope provided. Each book in this shipment has two entry coupons—and the more coupons you enter, the better your chances of winning!

© 1991 HARLEQUIN ENTERPRISES LTD.                    CPS-M1